Crabtree

a novel

Susan Zerlaut King

Crabtree; a novel by Susan Zerlaut King

ISBN 978-0-6450377-6-0

This edition first published in 2022 by immortalise
www.immortalise.com.au - info@immortalise.com.au

Typesetting and cover layout by Ben Morton

Cover art by Anna Rail
The House with the apple orchard, 2018
Watercolor batik on Japanese paper

To Mark Worthing,
a better mentor could not be found.

1

My forty-fourth birthday had been another ordinary day at the office. By late afternoon I was busy clearing my desk of paperwork that had accumulated over the past week. I'd started out with a clean desk, but as usual, I'd let the paperwork get away from me. It was nearly five o'clock on a Friday and I wanted nothing more than to finish up and head home for the weekend. Not that I had anything in particular planned; it was enough just to be away from the office for a couple of days. I was looking forward to a quiet evening at home with a drink and a good book. Or maybe I'd pop on the baseball game. The Tigers were playing.

That's when the phone rang and I decided to ignore it. Whoever was calling was going to have to wait until Monday.

But the caller was persistent and when the phone rang a second time I glanced at the caller ID. Janet and I talked often, but I doubted she was calling to wish me happy birthday. My sister knew well enough not to call me at work unless it was a matter of life and death.

In this case it was the latter.

My sister informed me our father had died that afternoon.

His death was a shock, even though he was elderly. And I was saddened by it. But, to be honest, I mostly felt anger; anger that a door had been closed, and there wasn't a thing I could do about it.

Gripping the phone tightly, I said, "I'll be there as soon as I can."

With resignation I returned to Brooks Creek, a small rural town in western Michigan. I'd grown up on a nearby farm where my father had had a small apple orchard, kept a few cows and grown a bit of corn and hay. The long drive had given me time to think, and my thoughts had become heavy with the difficult times I'd had growing up.

For years I'd hoped for a 'restart' with my father, but that had never materialized. I felt cheated, but that no longer mattered. I was going to have to accept there was nothing left to do but bury him.

The day of the funeral was the kind of spring morning that made people want to play hooky from work and go out for a run, or play their first round of golf for the year. The trees lining the street were leafing out after the long gray winter. Tulips, daffodils, and hyacinths that had only broken through the ground a few weeks before were now masses of yellow, red, and purple, giving the morning a festive feel. But for Janet and me it had been a long three days since the death of our father. It was difficult to feel the joy of spring.

I'd gotten up that morning and followed my usual routine. I showered and shaved, put on my suit and tied my tie, preparing for the funeral the same way I prepared to go to work every day. With nothing left to do before it was time to leave, I stood staring out the dirty motel window at traffic. It was a small town, but a surprising number of cars passed by as people hurried off to work, radios tuned to catch the early news and weather. I knew somewhere children were lined up at bus stops, and retirees had most likely already gathered at local cafes for breakfast. It seemed strange that life could go on as usual.

I heard the tires crunch the gravel as I pulled my Buick into the parking lot of the Brooks Creek Methodist Church. Two familiar vehicles were already parked in front. My sister's family had gotten there ahead of me. A black hearse was parked off to the side beneath a large maple tree. Two men in dark suits leaned against the vehicle holding cups of coffee. I considered whether this was just another routine day for them, as well.

Turning off the engine I decided to sit for a few minutes. Not for the first time, I wondered why people put themselves through things like this. I would have been satisfied with a simple burial.

It felt strange to once again be back at this church where for years as a child I'd attended services with my mother and Janet. My father hadn't gone with us. I never asked why; it was just the way things were. When my mother died thirty years ago, I'd never returned.

Gazing at the church was like seeing an old friend and being startled by how much they had aged, forgetting how much I'd changed as well. I certainly had, and not necessarily for the better.

Examining the church more closely I saw how much it had suffered over the years. Sitting in front of shimmering thirty foot pines, the once white clapboard building had turned to a weathered gray, and cracks in the stone foundation revealed signs of erosion. The cobbled roof, a patchwork of different shades of green, had been created by new shingles placed next to old ones over the years.

Several scrawny bushes were in need of replacement, but a few hardy spring bushes had survived and were in full bloom, most notably the lilacs which had been planted too close to the building. Rising nearly to the roof they leaned away from the church, a deep shade of purple flowers hanging down like clusters of grapes against the blue sky. But even with all its neglect, the old church still had about it an air of quiet beauty.

Finally I got out and stood next to my car, grateful for the stillness; few vehicles traveled the gravel road running past the church, leaving only songbirds to give voice to the morning. Blocking the sun with my hand, I raised my eyes to the steeple where the old brass bell was clearly visible. I wondered if they still rang it every Sunday.

I suddenly recalled the first time I'd been chosen to ring the bell to announce the start of service. I was eight years old and definitely a light weight; I could never gain enough weight to catch up with the other boys my age no matter how hard I tried. I'd never given much thought to ringing the bell.

My hands barely closed around the large, rough rope. I pulled down with all my might. Nothing happened. I tried again and again, but couldn't pull down hard enough to make the darned thing ring. Finally, the pastor smiled and said, "Let me get you started, Patrick. Hang on tight." He placed his large hands above mine and pulled. As he let go, I felt my feet leave the floor and heard the loud clang of the bell. I had momentum then. He laughed as I dropped and was pulled up again and again. Finally, he said, "That's enough now. Time for church."

Chapter 1

I'd barely heard what passed for service that Sunday. I kept reliving the feeling of being lifted off my feet, rising up like a bird taking flight.

I allowed myself a small smile. I hadn't thought about the bell in a long time

Bringing my eyes down to the double front doors of the church I saw they had been propped open. Just inside the pastor was talking to Janet and her family. As if this day wasn't already difficult enough, it was starting to get hot and humid. Pushing eighty degrees at ten o'clock in the morning was unusual for May in Michigan. I looked around the building hoping to see an air conditioner, but it appeared there wasn't any. I couldn't put it off any longer.

Approaching Janet, I saw her red, tear-rimmed eyes and the black pools of mascara that had formed beneath them. I felt a stab of guilt; I wondered if I'd been supportive enough of my sister. I wrapped my arms around her and pulled her close, feeling her body tremble. She was taking dad's death hard.

Janet stepped back and wiped at her eyes with one of the many tissues from the wad she kept twisting in her hands. She explained that we were going to wait in the pastor's office until everyone was seated. But after sitting and talking for three days that was the last thing I wanted to do. Her husband Phil could be overbearing even in the best of times. I knew I was too on edge to deal with him.

"I'd rather go in and sit, if that's okay?" I said.

Janet started to object, but Pastor Stratton must have seen something in my face. She reached over and touched Janet's arm. "That's not a problem. It'll only be a few more minutes until the service starts." Turning to me she added, "Patrick, you're welcome to wait in the sanctuary."

Taking the funeral card she offered I started up the familiar steps. At the top beneath a stained glass window sat a small table with an open Bible. Alongside it stacks of The Upper Room, a booklet of daily devotions were there for the taking. I was reminded of my mother who had always kept a copy on the nightstand next to her bed. I hesitated, then slipped one into my jacket pocket.

I entered the sanctuary and let the door close quietly behind me. I was alone. The only sound came from the hum of fans trying to circulate hot air. I made my way to the front pew and sat, worried that I might have hurt Janet's feelings. But I needed time to clear all the clutter out of my head that had accumulated over the past few days.

The sanctuary was much smaller than I remembered. There had been a few changes. The worn oak pews were now covered with thick red cushions. Those old wooden pews had been uncomfortable; so much so, that several of the elderly women had brought pillows to sit on. The wooden racks which held the Methodist hymnals were still attached to the back of each pew, their dark blue covers frayed around the edges. The old upright piano, the one that was always out of tune, was no longer in the corner; instead an electric organ stood in its place.

All around me hundred year old stained-glass windows let in the morning light. Vibrant reds, yellows, blues and pinks. I had always loved the way their reflected light spread over the sanctuary during morning service, just as it was then, enveloping us with rays of hope. In front of me, on either side of the altar, were two familiar prints of Jesus. On the left Jesus was depicted as a shepherd holding his staff surrounded by sheep; on the right he kneeled in prayer covered by a shaft of light. Above the altar hung a wooden cross.

Chapter 1

That was the view I'd had as a child every Sunday for years, before everything in my life went so wrong.

But there was one difference.

Now my father's casket was sitting in front of me.

I stared ahead at his coffin. No longer forced to face him in life, it was still difficult to face him in death. I was struggling to accept that we were there to bury him.

I didn't want to break down. I'd been holding myself together for days, but now I no longer seemed to have the strength, or the will, to continue. I squeezed my eyes shut against the tears growing there. I needed to get control. Taking a deep breath, I tried to calm myself, but I knew t it was too late. The battle had already been lost.

Thoughts began mounting of all the things I wanted to say. Needed to say.

About what we had lost. Of things that could have been.

Of how angry I was.

With tears flowing down my face, I said the only last words I could find.

"I'm here, Dad. Still struggling to talk to you, and finding only silence in return.

One last time."

Someone had slipped into the sanctuary unnoticed. Music began to play. Soft music to sooth the hurts, to comfort the weary. People began entering the sanctuary, and before long Janet, Phil and the girls came and sat beside me.

"Aren't the flowers beautiful?" Janet whispered nodding towards a dozen arrangements placed in front of us.

Honestly, I hadn't noticed.

As the service got under way, the shirt under my suitcoat started sticking to my back; my face and neck wet with sweat. Beside me Janet's damp hand squeezed mine. Behind me people fidgeted against the heat, waving whatever they could find across their faces, making rustling sounds to accompany the drone of fans. I hoped for a short service. I'm sure we all did.

Pastor Stratton opened with prayer. After a hymn and reading of the 23rd Psalm, it was time to speak about my father. Though never having met him, she told about life as a local orchard grower, a helpful neighbor, as a father to Janet and me. She related a couple anecdotes we'd told her about dad the day before. She'd asked, "Is there some fond memory of your father when you were growing up that you'd like to share with me?"

Janet's eyes slid towards me. She was worried about what I might say. I hadn't been prepared for the question. I'd pretty much been going through the motions trying to get through the day by agreeing with whatever Janet had wanted for the service.

Janet jumped in first. She always talked a lot when nervous, and began going on and on about fishing with dad. About their favorite fishing spot. The way he taught her how to bait a hook. Pastor Stratton kept nodding. "He liked to take me fishing for bluegills early in the morning" Janet said. "We'd bring our catch back home and mom would fry them up for breakfast."

"That sounds wonderful," Pastor Stratton had said smiling. Turning to me she asked, "And how about you, Patrick?"

My mind went blank. I searched for something, anything, to say. Finally, just as I used to do as a child, I blurted out the first thing that popped into my head. "He always let me have the last piece of pie."

Chapter 1

Maybe he had hoped I would start gaining weight and begin to fill out some.

Janet smiled and immediately I felt like such a fool. What a stupid thing to have said! The pastor must have wondered what kind of person would come up with something like that. I wanted to take it back and say something more meaningful, but it was too late. Pastor Stratton was already getting up. "It sounds like he was a generous man, Patrick." Patting me on the arm she told us she'd see us in the morning.

We turned to Amazing Grace in the hymnal. Thank goodness the service was coming to an end. Soon we were making our way on foot to the small cemetery behind the church where my mother lay buried.

As we walked I was reminded of happier times. I thought of Charlie and Buddy, my best friends. We had often gone to this cemetery at night. We'd made up wild stories—me being the biggest fabricator of ghosts and evil spirits—to scare each other or any girls we convinced to come along, while trying to convince ourselves that we had nothing to fear.

But there were no shadowy apparitions to terrorize us that day. The beautiful spring morning revealed nothing more than creamy-white spiraea and golden forsythia branches draped over the black wrought iron fence. The double gate was opened wide; its outstretched arms inviting us to enter. Only the calls of birds and the soft murmuring of people broke the silence as Janet and I walked arm in arm.

We continued the short distance to the back of the cemetery, passing a mix of new headstones and aged ones made unreadable by time and weather. Many dated back to the late 1800s. Some were barely visible standing amongst overgrown bushes.

My father's casket was suspended above the open grave and people assembled on either side of us. We stood behind my mother's headstone, making a semi-circle, as if we were trying to include her in my father's burial.

Pastor Stratton said a short prayer. The sound of rifles jolted me out of my thoughts. The veterans' honor guard from the local VFW was performing its duty, as they had for so many soldiers over the years. I felt Janet slip her arm around my waist. I placed mine over her shoulder and pulled her close as the mournful sounds of taps forced more tears from my eyes.

Then, just like that, the whole thing was over. One minute Janet and I were holding on to each other for support, the next, Pastor Stratton was inviting everyone back to the church basement for a luncheon prepared by the Ladies Aid. I wondered how we were supposed to just switch gears like that and suddenly have the desire for food and conversation after what had just taken place.

I told Janet to go ahead; I'd be along in a minute. I wanted to spend some time at mom's grave.

Once by myself I stood looking at my mother's headstone. 'Ellen Louise Crabtree, 1928-1979, Mother.' She'd been gone twenty-seven years.

I'd never stopped missing her.

Entering the church basement I saw a crowd of fifty people or so had formed two lines along tables covered with brightly flowered table cloths. The women of the Ladies Aid were scurrying back and forth to the kitchen adding more food to the already laden tables. Stacks of ham and egg salad sandwiches, potato salad, and bowls of colorful Jell-O covered one table, while lemon, apple, and cherry pies, and cakes of every flavor heaped the other. I saw my favorite, German chocolate, and realized I hadn't eaten since yesterday.

Snagging a piece of cake and a cup of black coffee I headed for one of the long tables set up with metal folding chairs. Janet was talking to a group of ladies on the other side of the room, but I hoped to sit by myself. I had no desire to make small talk.

Before I could sit someone tugged on my sleeve. I looked down at a round, gray haired woman. She wore a bright yellow dress stretched much too tightly across her middle. Something about her was familiar, but I couldn't place her. Had she been one of my teachers?

"Is that all you're going to take, Patrick?"

Not wanting to be rude I answered, "Well, for now. I'll get something else later."

"I'm so sorry about your father."

"Thank you," I said, as I placed the coffee and cake on a table and began undoing my tie and loosening my collar. The heat in the basement filled with so many people crowded together was even worse than it had been upstairs.

"I heard he had a stroke. Is that right?" she said standing much too close. Next to her nose a large mole with a long gray hair sticking out of it moved up and down as she talked. I thought of whiskers and tried not to stare.

"Yes, that's what happened," I said stuffing the tie in my pocket. She peered up at me blinking rapidly through her wire-rimmed glasses and I suspected she'd been designated to dig up gossip to share with her friends.

"I hope he didn't suffer. It's always hard to hear something like that. Was it fast then?" she asked. Why would she ask me something like that? I had no way of knowing. I began looking around for an escape.

"Yes, as far as I know," I replied.

"I keep thinking about Ed finding him like that. Poor man, he won't forget that for a while." She edged closer and I tried to take a step back from the pungent odor of sweat radiating from her body, but the table blocked me in.

"No, I'm sure he won't." I needed desperately to get away from this woman, before I lost my resolve to make it through the day without becoming churlish. I didn't want to talk about my father's death with her, or anyone else. I tried moving sideways along the table, but she moved closer and stood in my way.

She leaned towards me whispering in a conspiratorial tone, "Well, I guess it was a good thing he was sitting on his front porch when it happened, or who knows when anyone would have found him."

Ahh. Now I could see where she was going with this. Dad all alone. No kids around checking on him. Guilty as charged.

"With both of you gone, you know," she continued. "You and Janet living so far away, I mean. You're way off in Chicago, aren't you?

"Yes, well… I'm sorry, but you'll have to excuse me. I see my cousin and I really need to go talk to her." I made my escape then and headed to the other side of the room. There was no cousin, of course. Janet and I had no close relatives. On the way I downed the rest of my already cold coffee and dropped the empty cup into the trash bin along with the uneaten cake.

Chapter 1

Too much time away had made me an outsider. I didn't know, or at least couldn't remember, most of those people. I didn't want their condolences. They had no idea how I felt.

I waited as Phil and the girls said their good byes and started back to Lansing. Janet, however, was staying behind and planned to spend the next couple days with Mary Beth, her best friend. I was glad she wasn't going to be alone. Before she left we agreed to meet at dad's farm the next morning.

As I reached the exit Pastor Stratton was shaking hands saying, "Thanks for coming" and "God bless." I stood back until I had her alone. I could hear the clatter of dishes being washed in the basement and the hum of soft laughter between the women as they worked together putting everything in order. Pastor Stratton grasped my hand.

"Thank you for the nice service," I said.

"Patrick, please let me know if there's anything I can do for you."

I hesitated. I don't know what came over me, but I said, "Well, there is one thing."

"Of course, whatever you want, I'd be happy to help you."

Looking up wistfully at the rope hanging from the belfry, I asked, "I was just wondering...would it be all right if I rang the bell?"

Crabtree

2

The next morning after showering and listening to the news I found myself pacing anxiously in the cramped motel room, and decided to leave for the farm early. I drove slowly through the town of Brooks Creek, a town I normally bypassed on my way to see my father. I wasn't alone in that. It wasn't a town most people went out of their way to visit. Major shopping was usually done in Muskegon or other close-by cities with shopping malls and a diversity of restaurants.

While stopped at the only traffic light in town I glanced over at the old Ben Franklin store. Its uneven wood floors, jammed aisles, and large variety of merchandise had made it an interesting place to spend my allowance when I was young. What had caught my eye, though, were the displays in the large windows. The store had been transformed into an antique shop. Old lamps with fringed shades, china set out on a drop-leaf table, and a frilly hat hanging off a ladder back chair had been placed there to entice customers.

I thought of Nora. She would have loved going through the store with her fondness for old furniture, vintage clothing, and jewelry. She always knew how to put things together with pleasing results. I shook my head and pushed back my thoughts.

It was best not to dwell on Nora.

The light changed and I continued on. Near the end of town I was surprised to see Mr. Carpenter's drug store had been torn down and replaced with a new Rite Aid store. I was dismayed. I wondered what had become of Mr. Carpenter. He and I had spent a lot time together working in his store. He had helped me through a very rough time in my life, but that had been years ago. I hoped wherever he was, he was doing well.

Checking the gas gauge I decided I'd better fill up and pulled into the Wesco station across the street. Coming out of the station with a steaming cup of coffee I stopped to inhale the sweet smell of freshly cut hay, soon followed by a whiff of manure. Smells of my childhood. I found myself smiling as I got back in my car.

Before long I was passing Brooks Creek High School and caught a glimpse over the fence of students gathering for track practice. I was reminded of my short stint on the football team, a laughing matter now, though back then it had been quite traumatic. My memoires of high school, though, were mostly about my friends Buddy and Charlie. Like all teenagers we were going to conquer the world, but that turned out to be much more difficult than any of us had thought.

Ten minutes later I turned on to Abbott Road, a gravel lane that would take me to my childhood home. I passed rows of fragrant apple trees and began to feel my body slow down as the tension from the last few days eased from my shoulders and neck. There had been changes, but many things were still familiar, like dad's orchard.

But death wasn't familiar and Janet and I had decisions to make. I hoped it would only take a few days and we would have my dad's estate taken care of and could go back to our own lives. But as I pulled into the end of the driveway to the farmhouse and stopped, I wasn't so sure anymore.

Dad's mailbox was leaning precariously to the left and the door hung open, probably a victim of last winter's county snowplow. I got out, pushed it upright and gathered the mail. Dad's electric bill, The Weekly Shopper, and a few advertisements. I threw the mail on the passenger seat and proceeded up the driveway to the house, mud splattering against the sides of my car from puddles left by last night's rain. I turned off the engine and got out.

In the distance there was the sound of a cow bawling from behind the barn. Other than the ticking of my engine as it cooled, no other sounds made their way into the morning stillness. It seemed too quiet. Before me the apple orchard was in full bloom and wildflowers covered the scraggly front lawn. After Mom died Dad never really bothered much with taking care of the lawn.

The apple blossoms reminded me that spring had always been my favorite time of year, coming after a long hard winter. Spring meant more freedom for me, even though it meant the farm work greatly increased. Winter usually left us tied in knots. My father's personality had left no room for patience. In winter he'd pace back and forth in the kitchen, often stopping to stare out the windows towards the snow covered orchard. After an hour or two of this we were all left feeling tense. Mom would say, "For heaven's sakes, Sam, get out of my way. I can't get anything done with you moping around." He was like a fish in an aquarium, circling around with no place to go. In winter we were too confined for a family that seldom had much to say to each other.

We ate most meals around the kitchen table with little conversation. When my father did speak he had such a booming voice it made us wince in anticipation. Everything came out sounding like a command, or an accusation. We felt we must be guilty of something, but of what, we were often not quite certain.

When dad left to go to back to work there was a sigh of relief. The kitchen would again feel warm and inviting. The clang of the pots and pans as mom began cleaning up was a welcome sound. Mom would smile more and would chat away at us about nothing in particular. Though sometimes she would seem more withdrawn and we wondered what it was that dad had said that had upset her.

I leaned back against my car and took a good look at the farmhouse. Like the church, it had been neglected. White with dark green shutters and trim, it was badly in need of paint. Limbs from the large maple tree rested on its roof. The screened in porch that ran across the front of the house had small tears in the screen, and one of the porch steps was missing a board. Bushes on either side appeared to be dead.

Unlike the inside of the house, where in winter we felt cramped and underfoot, the porch had been our haven. From the first warm evening of early spring until the last days of late September when we started needing jackets and the sun set just after six o'clock, we inhabited that space.

Each of us had a spot that was ours alone. Janet and I usually sat curled up in cushioned chairs reading. Mom would be in a wicker rocking chair crocheting, her fingers flying as strings of soft colorful yarn took shape into a baby blanket for a new mother. Dad would be in the other rocker, content to just listen to the night sounds—the buzz of mosquitoes that had found their way on to the porch, the constant thump and flutter of moths as they flung themselves against the screen drawn by the light of the lamp, and wave after wave of frog voices that would suddenly erupt one night in celebration of spring and carry on in such excitement it was hard to talk over them.

Sometimes we would sit together and listen to it softly rain, or watch a thunderstorm move in over the barn. On the hottest of nights we'd stay late on the porch trying to escape the suffocating heat of the upstairs bedrooms until, one by one, we gave up and drifted off to bed.

I glanced at my watch. There was still some time before I expected Janet, so I took my coffee and sat down on the porch steps. Everything seemed just as my father had left it, including his tractor still hooked up to the spray tank by the shed—as if any moment he would walk out the door and head back to work.

I was lost in my thoughts when an old blue Dodge pickup came up the driveway and pulled in behind my car. A man in bib overalls and a John Deere cap got out. It was Ed Snyder, our nearest neighbor.

"Mornin', Patrick," he said. "I thought I might catch one a ya here this mornin'."

"Good to see you, Ed," I said reaching out to shake his hand. "Janet will be along in a few minutes. You've been a big help to us through all this. We really appreciate it."

"No thanks necessary," he said taking off his cap and wiping his brow. "Anyone woulda done it."

"I'm not so sure about that, Ed. My dad always thought a lot of you as a neighbor and I can see why."

"Well, like-wise," he said. He seemed unsure what to say next. Finally he added, "I hafta say, though, it was quite a shock."

"I can't imagine. I'm sorry it had to be you who found him."

"I dropped over that day to give your dad some mail that got left in my box by mistake. I figured he'd be takin' a break 'bout then.

He was sittin' like usual in his rocker with the newspaper on his lap. At first I thought he'd just dozed off, ya know, with Dolly next to him as always, so I—"

"Wait a minute. Who's Dolly?"

Ed seemed perplexed. "Ya don't know who Dolly is?" Did dad have a woman friend, I wondered, looking at him blankly.

"Well, let me introduce ya to 'er. She's out'n the truck."

He walked back to the truck and opened the passenger door. Out jumped a golden retriever, probably not more than a year old. Her glossy fur shimmered in the morning sun as she trotted up the driveway, passed me as if I were of no consequence, and continued up the steps to the screen door where she stood wagging her tail. This was obviously home.

"Where the heck did she come from?" I didn't know dad had a dog. I wondered why I hadn't seen her when I was here a couple of weeks ago.

"I was here the morning after the big frost and I never saw any dog," I said.

A look passed Ed's face. Somehow he wasn't surprised I didn't know about Dolly. "Well, she was probably locked up in the barn. If he was goin' out ta work in the orchard he left 'er in the barn so she wouldn't follow 'im and maybe get hurt. He'd of hated ta run over 'er with the mower. The night he was out sprayin' he probably didn't want 'er in the way followin' him in the orchard after dark."

"But why'd dad get a dog?" I was thinking about how we were never allowed to have pets. Perhaps he was having problems with people stealing. But she didn't look much like a guard dog.

"Well, it's more like the dog got him," Ed laughed. "A few months back he told me he got up one mornin' and found 'er lyin' by the porch steps. As ya'd expect, he told 'er to git out, but she never moved. I saw 'er later that day. She was a real mess. Her fur was matted, and covered with burrs and dirt. Underneath ya could tell she was some kinda yellow dog. We decided maybe she was one of them golden retrievers, a pup. No tags or nothin'.

He told me he'd left 'er ta go do his chores, but when he come back she was still there. He'd yelled at 'er some more. Said he didn't need no dog. Finally he decided maybe she was too weak to leave, so he filled a dish with some leftover goulash and give 'er some water. The dog just lay there the whole time with 'er head on 'er paws and looked at the dish. Didn't try ta eat nothin'. Later when he come back again the food was gone. I told 'im he was makin' a big mistake feedin' that dog. She'd never leave now."

Shaking his head, he started to chuckle, the wrinkles of his weathered face deepening, his light blue eyes reflecting the morning sun.

"I was right. The next day she was still there, though lookin' a bit perkier. She was sittin' up on 'er haunches instead of just lyin' there. In the dish I could see halfa hamburger. I had ta laugh. Yer dad was gonna have a dog whether he wanted one or not.

Well, a few days later when I stopped she looked like a whole new dog. Yer dad said she'd been followin' him out ta do chores and would swim in the pond behind the barn. She was a lot cleaner. He'd gotten out one of the combs he used ta use on the work horses years back and got the burrs outa 'er fur. I could tell he was gettin' attached, though he woulda never admitted it.

"Why did he call her Dolly?" I interrupted still having difficulty picturing my dad with a dog.

"Well, about two weeks later he got up one mornin' and found her lyin' by the porch steps, just like that first day. He said he looked closer and saw she'd gotten hurt somehow. She'd a badly mangled leg. He wondered what in the world she'd tangled with. He was afraid ta fix the leg himself 'cause of infection, ya know, so he put 'er in his truck and took 'er ta the vet where she got fixed up right proper." Ed stopped and laughed. "The vet wanted ta know what 'er name was. Yer dad had always called 'er Dog. He had ta think fast. He didn't want the vet ta think she was nothin' more'n a stray. He told the doc 'er name was Dolly. Why, I don't know. But she's been Dolly ever sense." Ed stopped and looked down at Dolly. "So that's how Dolly got 'er name and come ta live with yer dad."

I found this quite an amazing story, knowing my dad as I did. "Well, I agree, she's a beautiful dog."

"Anyway," Ed continued, "I'm not sure what ya want ta do with Dolly. She's a good dog, but I sure don't need another dog. Besides, she's not much of a farm dog, if ya know what I mean."

Dolly was sitting between us now. She looked up at me with pleading eyes.

"It's okay, Ed. She'll be fine here for a while until we figure something out. I'll be staying for a few days." I looked at Dolly, then scratched her between the ears. "It's okay, Dolly. I'm not much of a farm person myself. We'll get along just fine."

Dolly looked up at me and offered a paw.

3

I was still getting acquainted with Dolly when Janet arrived and we invited Ed in for coffee. As we entered the house there was a distinctive closed-up smell and something smelled rotten. I found the offending garbage can next to the refrigerator and took it out and set it by the back step. While I opened windows, Janet began brewing coffee and Ed gave her the short story on Dolly. I was glad I wasn't the only one who hadn't known about her. I cleared the clutter from the kitchen table as Janet washed some coffee mugs. Soon we were sitting around the kitchen table. Janet had found a few stale cookies in a tin with Christmas designs on the lid. If you dunked them in coffee first, they weren't so bad, especially if you hadn't eaten breakfast.

Ed's boys had been doing the chores since dad died and Janet asked if they could continue for a few days longer. She knew this was quite an inconvenience, but we'd pay them for their time and work. Thankfully Janet had made these arrangements right after she got the news about dad. I was hoping they would. I really had no desire to start milking cows twice a day, though I could do it if I had to.

"I've been thinkin' on those cows," Ed said, reaching for another cookie. "That's if ya plan on gettin' rid of 'em. I don't know if yer thinkin' 'bout keepin' the place or not."

Janet and I exchanged glances. I nodded. "Neither Janet nor I have any plans to keep the farm, so if you've thoughts on the cows, we'd be glad to hear them."

"I know a coupla' farmers might take 'em off your hands if ya want me to give 'em a call. I'd make sure they offered ya a fair price." He examined the cookie; then dunked it in his coffee.

"We'd appreciate any help you can give us. It's hard to know where to start with all this" Janet said with a swoop of her hand. "There's chickens, too. I'm not sure how many—maybe a dozen."

"Ya won't get nothin' for them chickens."

"Could you use a few more chickens, Ed?" I asked. "We'd gladly give them to you."

"Well, sure. Guess I could take 'em. They're leg-horns. A twitchy bunch, but good layers. I'll have the boys come over one night and get 'em." I looked puzzled, so he added, "They've been roamin' free for a few days now. Yer dad always let 'em out during the day, but locked 'em back up in the coop at night. Most of 'em are probably roostin' in trees by now."

Not sure how we would catch them in trees and not wanting to show my ignorance, I again thanked him for all he had done to help us.

"It's no problem. Yer dad was always one ta help me out any time I needed it. He was the best mechanic around, ya know. Many a time I was about ta give up on that ol' tractor of mine, but he'd come over and get it goin' again. Never would take any money for doin' it. I'm just returnin' the favor. That's what neighbors do."

After Ed left, Janet refilled our cups. Dolly had been pacing from room to room ever since we let her in the house. Now she was on her way upstairs.

"I think she's looking for dad," I said.

"I need to ask you something, Patrick," she said, her finger nervously tracing the flower pattern on the cup. "Do you think dad had a stroke because he got too riled up after your talk with him? I've been thinking that with his blood pressure and all maybe we'd done the wrong thing. He never did like anyone meddling in his affairs. I can picture him sitting here stewing away for days. Was he terribly upset when you told him we thought he should retire?"

"I'm sorry, but he was so exhausted that day from spraying all night, it didn't feel like the right time to bring it up. So, no, Sis, that had nothing to do with him dying. Besides, we both know he would've never agreed to it."

She seemed relieved. "I know. I shouldn't have asked you to do that. I guess I was feeling guilty about not getting out here myself to see him sooner."

"He would've been miserable if he quit farming. Could you see him sitting on the porch all day long staring at the orchard and doing nothing? It's probably better that it happened the way it did. At least he didn't end up in some nursing home. I can't imagine someone taking care of dad in a home."

"Me, either," she laughed. "That would not have been a pretty picture."

"But I wish now I'd talked to him more that morning," I said getting serious again. "After his stroke last winter I kept thinking I should try again to make things better between us. You know I've never been able to crack that streak of unforgiveness he had. Once you crossed a line with dad, he never forgave you. Now it's too late."

"Dad wasn't an easy person, that's for sure," she said. "What happened between the two of you has always made me sad. But

Patrick, he and I weren't close either."

"But he accepted you. You married a doctor and gave him grandchildren."

"Don't kid yourself. He barely knew his grandchildren's names. He seldom saw them. I'd invite him to come for the holidays, even offered to come and get him, but he always said no. He had things to do. When we came here to visit he walked around mumbling and grumbling, complaining about things that weren't getting done. The girls were a bit afraid of him for all his gruffness. We can't change who he was."

"That's true, but I wanted it to end better between us. I thought if he could finally see that I'd done what I set out to do with my life, become a writer; get a book published even, that he... Never mind. Just once in my life I wanted him to see me as successful, not some failure."

"You're not a failure and it wasn't fair the way he treated you, Patrick. Dad seemed to have a different set of standards for you than he did for me. Maybe it was because I was a girl, but he always seemed to expect more of you."

I could feel the old familiar anger returning. Dolly had come back downstairs so I reached over and smoothed the fur on the top of her head. I got up and followed her outside where I checked her water dish, then stood looking out over the orchard remembering the last time I'd seen my father.

I'd been to a conference that week in Detroit, then spent Saturday at Janet's house in Lansing. When I was packing up to head back to Chicago Sunday morning Janet asked me to stop and check on dad. It was May and she hadn't been to see him since late March.

I balked at the idea. Seeing dad always left me depressed. And worse, she wanted me to broach the idea of him retiring since he'd had a minor stroke just after Christmas. His health was poor, his pace grew slower each season, and he was always tired and cranky—but that was nothing new. He'd been alone for so many years since mom died it became more and more difficult to have a conversation with him. I told Janet that there was no way dad was going to give up farming, and I was the last person he'd take advice from. She asked me to at least try, so I found myself agreeing to stop at the farm on my way home, thinking what a disaster that was going to be.

That morning driving west down I96 towards Muskegon I was listening to the news on the radio. They were talking about the hard frost from the night before and how worried the orchard growers were. Many of the trees had started to bloom, and that made them vulnerable.

Dad listening to the news that night and hearing the frost warnings would've headed straight out to fill the spray tank with water; there was no need for chemicals. He'd put on his vinyl large brimmed hat and heavy rain coat and make his way to the orchard. Then he'd spend the rest of the night driving through the orchard to cover blossoms with hope-filled water, returning again and again to fill the tank—until sunrise. It was a method often used during a hard frost; spraying the trees with water to protect the blooms like a blanket when the water turned into layers of ice.

I had sometimes helped dad spray on those frosty nights when I was old enough. I would relieve dad during the night so he could get a bite to eat and fill up on coffee to stay awake; and staying awake was a problem. The rumble of the tractor engine and the roar of the sprayer could easily lull you to sleep. Many times I had started to nod off, only to have my head come up with a jerk, narrowly missing a tree, or the turn at the end of a row.

The radio said they predicted eighty percent of the crop was destroyed. That was a lot of work done without much reward.

I found dad that morning, head on his arms, asleep at the kitchen table, cold plate of eggs and potatoes pushed to the side. With his dirty white hair hanging down to his whiskered face, he looked every bit of his eighty years. On the stove were the uneaten leftovers of last night's supper—beans and potatoes cooked together in a cast iron skillet. I filled a mug with cold coffee from the coffee maker on the counter. The ding of the microwave roused him from his sleep.

"Patrick?" he said, a bit of confusion on his face.

"Yeah, it's me, Dad. I didn't mean to startle you."

I warmed him up a cup of coffee and offered to make him a new breakfast, but he declined. We sat and talked about the crop loss. He seemed resigned. He told me it was a gamble farmers take every year. I sensed his weariness though was from more than just lack of sleep. It had to be difficult looking at all that was lost after so much work, not to mention the financial loss. There would be little apple crop to harvest that fall to cover the cost of all the spraying he'd already done.

I just couldn't get up enough courage after that to talk to him about retiring. He seemed defeated and I didn't want to add to his worries. Janet would have to understand. This was what dad would do, until he couldn't do it any longer.

I decided to change the subject. I'd tell him about something happening in my life.

Chapter 3

"Well, I've gotten some good news. I'm going to have a book published soon." I worked as an insurance agent, a job I hated, but it paid the bills. When I wasn't working I did what I loved to do most. I wrote. I was always scribbling ideas in notebooks or on slips of paper to use later. I'd had some articles and a couple of short stories published, but this was my first novel. After all these years of writing it was exciting, but I was also feeling a bit of anxiety. This was an important undertaking, and I hoped I was up to the challenge.

He nodded, showing little interest. I might as well have commented on the weather. So I repeated myself. "Dad, I'm getting a book published."

Finally he asked, "What's it about?" Maybe I was expecting congratulations? If so, there didn't seem to be any forth coming.

Well, that was going to be hard to explain, especially to my father. It was about a man in his thirties who wanted nothing more than to be an artist, but was caught up in the computer age working for a software company. He was continually trying to find a way to devote his life to painting instead. Then he met a woman who changed his life in ways he never could've imagined. But all wasn't as it seemed. It was sort of a love-hate relationship with technology, the world of art, and the woman he loved. How could I explain that to my dad who still used a landline phone and listened to the news on the radio?

"It's hard to explain. I'll send you a copy."

He nodded, but I knew he'd never read it. After all, a while back I'd sent him a copy of the Chicago Magazine. They had published a short article I wrote called, "Life on the River Walk". It had a small photo of me wearing a cap and sunglasses sitting at a table with my notebook and cup of coffee, observing people as they strolled by on a Sunday morning. The caption read, "Writer Patrick Crabtree gains inspiration for his characters from watching people on the River Walk." Dad had never mentioned it. He'd probably just thrown it away.

By noon I was back on the road.

4

Back inside the house Janet had refilled our coffee mugs. I sat down across from her and tried to focus on what lay ahead.

"Patrick, we haven't had time to talk about the farm. I'm hoping we can make some decisions today. Personally, I think we should sell it. When we were talking to Ed it seemed we were both in agreement that neither one of us wanted the farm. I mean, I don't want it, do you? I want to make sure we're both on the same page."

"Don't worry, we are. I can't picture myself living here," I answered quickly. And I really couldn't. The thought had never even entered my mind. But now thinking about strangers living in our childhood home I suddenly felt a tug of nostalgia. It was hard to imagine people sitting in our kitchen drinking coffee talking about their day. The plans they would make to change the house. My mom's décor replaced by someone else's ideas. My parents replaced by different people next to the fireplace at night. But I needed to be realistic. The farm was no place for me, and I knew it.

"Let's put it up for sale, Janet."

"Okay, then. I want to know what you think about this plan. Before I left this morning I talked to people at my bank. They suggested we consider setting off the house and five acres separately from the farmland. The house might sell faster, provided we can get it in shape. There are people who want a place to live in the country without having to farm. Maybe keep a few chickens and a couple of horses for the kids to ride. And then there are farmers who just want to add acreage to their farms. The land here is good farmland. I don't think it'll be hard to sell."

I'd known all along that we'd have to do something with the farm eventually, but I hadn't really given it much thought. I didn't really expect to be making these decisions so soon. But Janet wasn't wrong to be thinking about all this. There really wasn't any reason to wait. In good old Janet-style she had taken some initiative and was way ahead of me on this. Selling really was the only thing we could do.

"Well, we'll need to contact the township about splitting the land, and a real estate agent about selling the house...once it's ready. I know there's going to be a ton of work to do here first," she said. "And I can put an ad in the paper for the land. See if we get any offers. If not, we'll have to list that as well. Of course, we'll have to get rid of all the farm equipment and things from the house. It might be easiest to call an auctioneer."

She'd obviously been thinking about all the details, but I hadn't had any experience with auctioneers either. Why hadn't I thought about all this before and left it all to Janet? Now I was in over my head. My face must have shown some concern.

"It's not going to be that difficult, Patrick. People do it all the time. Why don't we spend the rest of today going through the house and the other buildings and see what's what. That might give us some idea of how long this is all going to take."

She took off her glasses and put them on the table revealing the dark circles beneath her eyes. "I can only stay two more days, Patrick. After that I'll have to get back to work. I talked to my boss and I can start taking Fridays off so I'll be able to have longer weekends to help sort out everything. But I can't do this all by myself; and you can't drive here every weekend from Chicago either. I'm not sure how we're going to handle this."

"I wouldn't let you do it by yourself, Janet." I was wondering myself just how long this was going to take. I had a month's worth of vacation time coming, but I knew my boss wasn't going to like it one bit. It was hard enough to get a couple days off, let alone a month, but it was owed me and I needed to take it. We were always running behind at work, but he would just have to handle things without me for a while. Still I dreaded the call. "I'll take my saved up vacation time. I have at least a month's worth."

"That would really help a lot."

"This couldn't have happened at a worse time, Janet. I'm right in the middle of editing my manuscript. It's time consuming. I'll have no choice but to dedicate some my time here to working on it. My editor's going to be contacting me about changes I need to make. He'll expect me to be available."

Thinking about my book and all that would have to be done to settle the estate, I felt the pressure begin to mount. This whole thing was already overwhelming. And we hadn't even started.

"I understand, Patrick. And by the way, congratulations!" she said getting up and giving me a hug. "With all that's been going on I haven't had a chance to tell you how proud of you I am."

We toured the house room by room, while I wrote notes on a pad of paper. It wasn't long before we began realizing just how much work we were in for. Plumbing was going to be a big issue. The downstairs toilet didn't flush well and the faucets in both bathrooms dripped. There were half a dozen floor tiles in one of the bathrooms that had come loose. Looking beneath them it was apparent there'd been a small flood at some point; part of the floor was rotten and was going to need replacing. Well, it was something I was capable of doing. Maybe take me a day or two.

Moving on to the kitchen we discovered a leak under the sink as well. Dad had set a pan under it, which was running over on to the floor. After emptying the pan we examined the rest of the kitchen. The cupboards were desperately in need of new paint and the rest of the kitchen thoroughly scrubbed. Okay, I thought, maybe we'd need a week.

Janet started opening the cupboards to see what was inside. "We can give these dishes to Good Will," she said. "The pots and pans, too. They might as well go to people in need. And here, we can throw out all his medicine." She picked up a bottle and read the label. "Look at this. This is the medicine he was given at the hospital after his stroke."

"So?" I said.

"So, it's still full. He never took it."

I shook my head. "Why am I not surprised?"

"That makes me angry. Maybe he didn't need to die, Patrick."

"You know how stubborn he was. You couldn't tell him anything. I'm sure his doctors had the same problem."

"All the same, he didn't even try to get better. I wish I'd known."

"We probably couldn't have convinced him to take it either. There's nothing we can do about it now."

We moved outside. The sagging porch steps needed to be rebuilt. The handrail that had been installed to help support my mother now leaned precariously to the left, no longer safe. Walking around the house we observed windowsills that were bare of paint and a pane of glass broken in one of the living room windows, the pieces held together with clear packing tape. I dragged out a ladder and got up on the roof, which made me nervous. Unlike dad, I was never good with heights. The roof seemed okay to me as far as I could tell, but we would have to get someone to trim the maple tree limbs off the house.

Back on the ground we knew the lawn was going to need a lot of attention. Years of dead leaves from the large maple tree in the front yard had gathered up against the sides of the house. Most of the bushes were dead. Surprisingly, Mom's old climbing rose bush was still hanging on. It was straggly, but bits of green showed here and there. The bush used to climb a wooden trellis, but that was nowhere in sight.

"That bush always had the most beautiful clumps of pink roses," Janet said with the hint of a smile. "Looks pretty bad but let's see if we can save it. I think it just needs to be pruned back. It's worth a try." I nodded, thinking we'd better set aside two weeks.

We didn't know if there was a lawn mower anywhere, so we headed over to the tool shed to look for one. Dad's white Ford pickup truck was parked in front by the gas pump. It was ten years old, full of rust, with a badly dented tailgate and cracked windshield. The whole truck was covered with layers of dried mud. A chainsaw, pruners, and gas can were in the back. The driver's door was ajar so I closed it; then we stepped into the shed. We were quickly hit by the smell of oil, paint, and turpentine. Every tool was in place just as they always were. Dad had been a stickler about his tools and once you were chewed out for not returning a tool to its proper place, you never again forgot to put something you had borrowed back where it belonged.

Squinting into the darkness we saw a lawn mower in the corner behind a spare tire and a pair of wooden saw horses. I brushed away cobwebs and dragged it out into the sunlight. It was so covered in dust and grime I didn't think it had seen action for several years. I hoped I could get the darn thing going. Janet said not to worry. There was money in dad's account that we could use to buy things we needed for repairs.

Janet wanted to take a quick look at the barn. It was old, but dad had done his best with the upkeep. Someone buying the place may want to do some things, but I thought we should just let that be. Janet agreed. She quickly wrote down equipment in the barn and in the sheds to discuss with an auctioneer. She said once we were ready the auctioneer would come out and list everything, but this would give him an idea of what we had. Any furniture in the house we thought might bring a price we could put out on the lawn to be auctioned off, though neither of us thought there would be much. "Really," she said, "most of the furniture can just be donated or thrown out once the house is sold."

"We haven't checked the basement or the attic," she said sounding tired. We trudged back to the house and made our way down the steep basement stairs into the dampness. Our footsteps disturbed a mouse which scurried off to a hiding place behind the furnace. The single overhead light bulb revealed a basement overflowing with things collected and discarded over the years. There were several boxes of empty canning jars, a couple large crocks, a few old, moldy Woman's Day magazines, and half dozen or so smaller wooden boxes filled with nuts, bolts and screws. Shoved together stood a mixture of other unwanted items. A broken chair, a lamp with no shade, an old wagon of mine that was missing a wheel, a wooden stool with peeling blue paint, and a stack of frayed tarps full of holes. Everything was covered with thick layers of dirt. Over the years spiders had connected all the clutter together with a sheer blanket of webs. I wondered how long ago anyone had been down there. I stopped trying to figure out how long this all was going to take.

My attention was drawn back to the canning jars. I remembered them filled and sitting on shelves with the things my mother canned from the garden. There had been no end of tomatoes, beans, beets, corn, peaches, plums, and applesauce, sitting next to jars of colorful homemade jam. Before we got our big freezer we even canned meat. Dad would buy a steer from a neighbor and have it butchered. Then we'd spend days filling and processing canning jars with beef. The meat was always so tender. I'd never tasted anything like it since.

Canning was a time-consuming event that lasted most of the summer and into the fall. Once things started ripening Janet was usually by mom's side helping to pick the produce and with the canning as well. The savory aroma in the kitchen lasted all summer, making it impossible to just pass through without stirring up thoughts of your next meal. I visualized my mom standing at the stove over the pressure cooker, sweat running down her face, her light brown hair in wet ringlets about her neck as she unsuccessfully tried to keep it pinned up. She often wore an apron that pulled over her head and tied in the back. I remembered one in particular, a white apron with bright red strawberries and a green ruffle around the edges.

Looking over at the crocks made me think of pickles. The crocks had always been full of them. I was crazy about sweet pickles and often would steal down to the basement to help myself to a handful, eating them on the spot, sweet pickle juice running down my chin, fingers sticky as I reached in for more.

Janet must have been having similar thoughts. "Wasn't it wonderful opening one of those jars in the middle of a cold snowy day?"

"It's something I'll never forget," I said feeling sentimental. "It's funny; looking at these things brings back so many memories."

"Yes, for me, too," she said softly.

After a moment I asked, "Is there anything you want to keep from here?"

"Not really. I certainly don't have the time to can anything. But canning jars are always in demand, so let's put those out for the auction. Did you see anything you want?"

"I'd like to keep the crocks. I'm not sure why or what I'll do with them. Maybe I'll use them for storage. I really don't have room in my apartment for anything that will take up a lot of space."

"The rest of this stuff can be thrown out then," Janet said taking one last look around.

"I'm thinking we should get a dumpster," I said. "It would make things easier." She agreed that we probably wouldn't have much trouble filling one.

We left and made our way up to the attic, both worried about what we would find there. It was a similar situation to the basement. At first glance there seemed to be nothing but more junk to dispose of. It made me wonder why anyone had kept half the things stacked there without rhyme or reason, plunked down wherever available space could be found. Before long I heard Janet laugh. She had found a box of old toys and taken out a doll she remembered. "I'd like to keep this," she said setting it aside. A few minutes later I came across a chess set in a wooden box. Odd, I didn't remember anyone in our family ever playing chess. Maybe it had belonged to my grandfather.

Amongst the rest of the clutter was a pair of gray-green lamps —the metal frames of the shades pitted with rust, a baby high chair with a decal of a little lamb on the back, and a dress maker's dummy. A moth-eaten wool hunting coat in red plaid had been draped over its shoulders. A half dozen or so boxes of white dishes with a blue motif were wrapped in yellowed newspaper and stacked off to the side. Janet said the dishes had been Grandma Crabtree's. I recognized the pattern as similar to bowls in the kitchen that we had used for years.

None of the rest of the boxes in that area contained anything worth saving so we moved over to one of the darker corners. Piled there were several dilapidated boxes with tangled Christmas tree lights and decorations spilling out onto the floor. We cleared the mess out of the way to see what was behind them. In the gloom was an old ornate trunk pushed up against the wall. It was made of dark wood with rusty metal trim and hinges. We wondered if it was locked as there was no sign of a key. Looking at each other we knew we were both feeling the same way; we were kids who had just discovered a 'treasure chest'.

We brushed off the trunk and tested the lid. It opened with a loud creak. There years ago, wrapped in a white cotton sheet, my mother had tucked away her wedding dress and matching hat.

"Oh, Patrick, look at this," Janet said running her hand over the satin fabric. "It's so beautiful."

I knelt beside Janet looking at something I'd never seen before; something that had been treasured by my mother. I asked Janet if she had seen it before, and she shook her head. Gently she took out the dress so we could see it better.

"I think she made this herself. Look at all the tiny stitches. That must have taken quite some time." I reached in and pulled out the hat and placed it on Janet's head as she stood holding the dress in front of her. We both started to laugh. "I'd forgotten how small mom was," she said.

"You'll have to keep this, Janet. What would I do with it?" Janet carefully returned the dress and hat to the trunk and closed the lid saying she would take them home with her another time. She couldn't wait to show them to her daughters. We moved on followed by the smell of old mothballs that lingered in the air.

Ten minutes later I found myself standing in the middle of the attic thinking we were never going to get through all this. We'd be there a year. I nodded at a couple boxes on a small folding table. "Let's check those out, and then push everything for the auction into the center of the room. Later on I'll carry out the rest to the dumpster when we get one."

The brittle yellowed tape had long ago given up trying to keep the boxes sealed. We could see their exposed contents and let out a sigh. On the outside of the boxes someone had clearly written 'photos' and 'letters'.

"These may take some time to sort through," I said. "I'll take them downstairs and go through them later." I stacked one box on top of the other and made for the stairs. After placing them on the dining room table I looked at Janet and knew neither of us had the energy left to do any more that day.

Half an hour later and Janet was getting ready to return to Mary Beth's house. She intended to stay there when she came back on weekends as well. "I can't wait to take a shower," she said tucking strands of hair back into her pony tail and brushing aside a bit of cobweb from her shirt. There were streaks of dirt on her face and arms, and dark smudges on her jeans. I was sure I probably looked much the same. I walked with her out to her car, but instead of getting in she hesitated.

"I'm worried about you, Patrick," she said. "You can't keep staying at the motel. That's just too expensive. Do you think you'd be okay staying here? It's up to you. It's just a suggestion."

I didn't answer right away. Janet was aware of the depression I had fought off and on most of my life. But I'd already been giving it some thought. She was right, a month at a hotel really would add up. It made sense for me to stay at the farm.

"I'll be fine here," I said, though I wasn't sure how I really felt.

After Janet left I grabbed my car keys and headed for town to check out of the motel. Afterwards I stopped at Clauson's grocery store, a store that was a throw-back to simpler times. It was so different from the stores I normally shopped at in Chicago with all their exotic choices. Not knowing how much to get I settled on just a few items to start. I picked up a frozen pizza, some sandwich items, and a few things for breakfast, plus a six pack of beer. Then I thought of Dolly and got some dog food. I had no idea what Dolly normally ate. Probably dad's leftovers.

By the time I returned to the farm and carried in the groceries and my belongings it was already beginning to get dark. Dolly was happy to see me. I'd left her in the house, afraid she might run off looking for dad. After putting things away I prepared to bake the pizza, only to discover the oven didn't work. "Of course, it doesn't," I said slamming the oven door shut. The whole day had been about nothing but things that needed fixing; why should this be any different. Frustrated I settled for making a quick sandwich and sat down at the kitchen table with a beer.

Anxiety was beginning to creep in. I really didn't want to be there; I just couldn't think of a better alternative. It felt strange to be in the house alone. I'd been okay when Janet was there, but now the house seemed so empty. Even though I'd grown up there I still felt like an intruder. I kept feeling that if I turned around I'd catch Dad stepping in the door, surprised to find me sitting there.

As I ate I listened to all the unfamiliar sounds. Outside birds were making their last call to the day gone by; frogs and insects had begun taking over the night. Inside Dolly tried to get the last morsel out of her dish as it slipped and banged against the screen door. From a bottom cupboard came skittering sounds I interpreted as a mouse on the prowl. Gasps and shudders erupted from the old refrigerator as it tried to keep pace with the call for cooler temperatures while the clock on the wall loudly ticked away the night. It had grown quite dark in the kitchen except for the overhead light that cast large shadows into the corners.

After a while I became aware of two separate people sitting at the table. One was the successful Chicago business man, the one who had just written a novel; the other was the young boy who had sat at this same table years ago and dreamed of a different kind of life for himself, but had been stymied at every turn. Back and forth they jostled as memories from the last twenty years worked their way to the surface.

When I finished I put my dishes in the sink and turned off the kitchen light. It was fully dark now. I'd forgotten how dark it got in the country. I hadn't slept anywhere without street lights for a long time. I made my way to the stairs leading up to my old bedroom, retracing my steps from many years ago.

I found clean sheets in the linen closet, then after a shower I climbed into bed. I decided to read for a while, not yet ready to turn off the light, when I heard Dolly's nails clicking on the steps. Soon she appeared in the doorway where she stopped and stood staring at me. I realized Dolly was still missing dad.

"It's okay, Dolly. You can come in." A couple tail wags, but she didn't move; her eyes searched the room.

I slapped the mattress beside me. "Come, girl," I called. She ran across the room, jumped up on the bed, and laid next to me with her head on my stomach. As I gently stroked her, she looked up at me with her soft brown eyes. A few minutes later she heaved a sigh and settled down to sleep. It had been a long day for both of us.

5

The next morning I woke to an unaccustomed quiet; then I saw the softly snoring dog sprawled out next to me taking up a good two thirds of the bed. "Dolly, you stink—if you're going to sleep with me you'll need to take a bath."

The clock showed a little after six. I made my way down to the kitchen and fixed some coffee. Janet wasn't coming until nine so I decided to go for a walk. I slipped on a jacket and left with a mug of coffee, Dolly by my side. I hadn't gone far when she turned around and headed back towards the house. I shrugged. I guessed she didn't want to go with me after all; but then she reappeared with a tennis ball in her mouth and dropped it at my feet.

"Well, now. What's this? You want me to throw it?" I pitched it up the lane. She caught the ball on the second bounce. I was amazed. Not only did my dad have a dog, but it appeared he must have played with her as well. I couldn't remember a time he'd played catch with me.

I continued throwing the ball for a while, then put the slimy thing in my jacket pocket. "That's enough for today, Dolly. Let's cut through the orchard." We wandered up and down rows of apple trees getting our feet wet with dew. It felt good to be out in the early morning with only the birds keeping us company. I stopped and pulled down a branch to examine the blossoms. Black in the center. I pulled down another and another. All black. All dead. I wondered if there would be any apples at all that year. I hated to go back to the house, but I knew we had a long day ahead of us and should fix myself some breakfast before Janet got there.

Janet arrived as I was finishing my dishes. We had a quick coffee together while we planned what we'd do first. We decided she would start sorting things upstairs in dad's bedroom as I made lists of supplies I'd need to make repairs. Around noon she came down with a couple heavy garbage bags filled with some of dad's clothes and let them drop to the kitchen floor. She looked tense. Brushing the hair from her eyes she said, "These are dad's work clothes. I don't think we should donate them. I doubt we could ever get the chemical smells out of them."

"Yeah, I can smell them from here."

"And, Patrick," she said. "There's something else." I could see she was trying to hold back tears.

I put down my pad and pen. "What's wrong?"

"It's dad's closet. It's full of mom's clothes."

"You've got to be kidding me."

"Remember dad wouldn't even talk about mom after she died. He wouldn't let us touch anything that was hers. He said he'd take care of it. Well, obviously he didn't. Everything that was hers is still there. I had no idea he'd kept everything."

"What do you want to do?"

"We've no choice but to throw them out. They're outdated and some of the material is so old it just tears when you try to take it off the hanger. This is a whole lot harder than I thought it would be." She hunted for a tissue in her pocket and began wiping at her eyes.

"That's just great. Not only do we have to deal with dad's stuff, now we have to go through mom's things some twenty years later." I was getting angry. "I can help if you want. What I'm doing now can wait until later."

"That's okay. I don't think I'm up to it right now, but I can do it tomorrow. For now, I think I'll just find a different job to do."

As we returned to work I thought about mom's clothes still hanging in the closet. What a shock that must have been when Janet opened the closet door and saw them. I wondered how dad could open the closet door, day after day, year after year, and see mom's clothes still hanging there next to his. Had he held on to them for sentimental reasons? I'd never thought of him as a sentimental person. Maybe it was some form of denial. Or perhaps after putting it off for so long her clothes had become common place to him over the years. I didn't understand him at all and was angry he'd left them for us to sort through.

The following day was more of the same. We were beginning to get a better sense of how much there was to do and I began to worry that even a month might not be enough time. My boss, though not happy, had understood my request for time off. I got along with him okay. Better than my former boss, who happened to be my ex-father-in-law. But even so, I knew Jack would never agree to more time off if I asked. I hated to think I might end up having to drive back from Chicago on weekends to get things finished.

In the afternoon some good news came our way from Ed. He'd kept his word and brought us an offer from two different farmers for the cattle.

"They wanna split the herd between 'em," he said. "Six cows each." We agreed to the price even though neither of us had any idea what cows were going for. We decided to trust Ed. Come Saturday it would be a relief when they came to get them. One less problem. So far, so good, I thought.

After Janet left and headed back to Lansing, I wasn't up to doing any more work. I made a couple burgers and took them out to the porch along with a beer and sat at the small table. It was quickly becoming my favorite place in the house. It was usually full of light as opposed to the darkness of the rest of the house. The porch had been painted yellow and had a wide pine plank floor. Green gingham ruffles above the windows and matching cushions on the chairs my mother had made had long since faded. Pots of geraniums and petunias once lined the window ledges in the summer, but now they were bare. But even without the plants and bright colors, it was still a cozy place. Or maybe it was the memories.

I'd taken one of the boxes from the attic with me—the one marked 'photos.' As I ate and drank I began pulling out old photographs. There was one of my Aunt Edna, dad's only sister. I had only met her once when I was very young. She lived in Oregon and passed away a few years back. There were several photos of Janet at various ages, some with mom, and later some with me. Janet was three years older than me. There was a photo of her sitting next to mom on the couch holding me when I was a newborn. I wondered what she had thought of me back then. I set it aside to give to her when she came on Friday.

I took my dishes to the kitchen and set them in the sink, then returned to the porch where I continued through stacks of photos. There were pictures of the farm, a photo of dad with a long string of fish, and one of mom in the garden holding a very large watermelon. Some photos didn't have names on the back and I had no idea who the people were. I'd have to ask Janet about them.

Reaching in for another handful of photos my eye caught a small blue envelope. There was nothing written on the front. Carefully I removed the contents exposing a piece of paper and a faded black and white photo. It was of a small child. The paper was folded and coming apart where it had been creased. Unfolded I realized it was an official document of some kind. I tried to make sense of what I read. Puzzled, I read it again.

I was upset. I was sure Janet hadn't known anything about it either. She would have told me. I reached for my phone to call her, but hesitated. I decided to wait until she came on Friday. I wanted to see her reaction when I handed it to her.

My hands were shaking as I returned everything back to the envelope.

6

The next morning Dolly and I headed out for another walk. After a few rounds of chase the ball, I decided to take the lane behind the barn into the fields. Dolly was thrilled by my choice. She terrorized a couple of rabbits, then ran ahead and came back to me again and again, stopping to sniff along the way. I would lose sight of her from time to time in the tall alfalfa, then locate her by the flag of her tail. I couldn't help but wonder at her sense of abandon. I envied her.

After breakfast I picked up my list of supplies needed for repairs. It was cool enough that I thought Dolly could go with me and wait in the car. I opened the porch door and said, "Want to go for a ride?"

She was out of the house in an instant. Instead of stopping by my car, though, she ran past it and sat down next to the passenger side of dad's orchard truck.

"Well, I guess you've done this before, too," I said.

I opened the door and with little effort Dolly jumped up onto the seat. I walked around to the other side and got in, happy to see keys in the ignition. The truck was a mess. The dash and floor were littered with yellowed receipts. Various tools, loose nuts, bolts, and screws, along with greasy rags and ragged gloves were tossed about. I started the engine and smelled the strong odor of oil as a puff of black smoke exited the back of the truck.

Glancing over at Dolly I saw a bag of lemon drops on the seat next to her. Dad had sure loved his lemon drops. I reached over taking one out of the bag and popped it in my mouth before putting the bag in the glove compartment. No sense in leaving temptation in Dolly's way.

We bounced along down the driveway, Dolly riding shot gun with her head hanging out the window. I smiled. I wondered if my dad had felt the same way when Dolly rode with him. It was strange to imagine.

I spent an hour pushing a cart through Ace Hardware collecting things from my list. I'd done repairs like this before, but it had been awhile. I hoped I wasn't forgetting something. At least the hardware wasn't far from the farm. I remembered the mice and added mouse traps to the cart and headed for the checkout. I returned to the truck to find Dolly barking at a black lab sitting in the driver's seat of a pickup parked next to us.

"Find yourself a boyfriend?" I asked handing her a dog biscuit from the bag and receiving a sloppy kiss in return.

Once back at the farm I spent the rest of the morning, and most of the afternoon, attempting to fix the plumbing under the kitchen sink. Everything was old and hard to get apart. I was blinking away flakes of rust and drops of cold water from my eyes as I lay on my back, head stuck under the sink looking up at the offending pipes, when the phone rang. I was spitting out epitaphs by the time I had crawled out to answer it. It was Ed.

"Patrick, catch ya at a bad time?"

"Not at all, Ed," I lied. Then added, "I needed a break."

Chapter 6

"Would tonight be good for nabbin' them chickens?"

"Sounds good to me, Ed."

"The boys'll be along 'bout dusk," he said.

I'd not met Ed's sons as yet. Ed and his family bought the farm next to ours after I'd left home. They came every day in the early morning and late afternoon to do the chores, then would disappear without a word. Sometimes I'd only see the back of their truck as they drove off down the driveway. I kept meaning to get out and talk to them.

As it turned out, Ed's boys were about thirty, six foot four, three hundred fifty pounds give or take an ounce or two, wearing dirty bib overalls and stained white t-shirts. They introduced themselves as Henry and Ed, who was better known as Junior.

"We'll check the coop first. See what's what," Henry said. "But you'd better make sure Dolly's locked up inside. No need spookin' them chickens if she gets a mind ta start in barkin.' "

I took care of Dolly and then returned to the coop to watch. There was quite a ruckus coming from inside. Soon the 'boys' emerged, each carrying a chicken upside down in either hand by the legs.

"Just four in there," Henry said. They put the chickens in a cage in the back of their pickup truck. Next they took out two flashlights and two wooden poles about six feet long, each with a large metal hook on the end.

"Let's go find us them other chickens," Junior said. "Time ta check out the trees." I wanted to check out the trees, too. I wanted to know what they were planning. It was a bit like being on a safari as I followed my guides into the darkening orchard behind the coop, each one carrying a pole and a light.

They began flashing their lights in the trees searching for roosting chickens. Finally, Henry said, "Got one." I looked where he was shining his light halfway up a tree. Almost out of sight amongst the apple blossoms a white chicken perched with its head tucked under a wing, totally unaware of what was about to happen. Henry handed me his light. "Keep that on the chicken so I can see what I'm doin'." Carefully he slipped the long pole through the branches making as little disturbance as possible. Suddenly the sleeping chicken was yanked off its perch. It came squawking out of the tree, wings flapping, hanging upside down with the hook securely around its legs.

"I'll just put this one in the truck. You and Junior keep lookin'." He handed me his pole.

That was pretty slick I thought.

Three trees down we spotted another chicken about ten feet up. "You wanna nab it?" Junior asked.

Well, of course I did. Putting down my light I began slipping the pole through the branches. "I can't see the legs," I complained. Junior adjusted his light a bit and yellow legs appeared. Cautiously I moved the hook closer. I thought I had the thing, but when I yanked, it soon became apparent I had only hooked one leg. The chicken squawked and freed itself, flying off to another tree.

"Don't worry 'bout it," Junior said. "We'll let it settle and come back for it later."

It was full dark now. Stars were filling the sky as we stalked our prey. On the fifth tree another chicken sat roosting.

"Go ahead," Junior said. "You've gotta get at least one." And I did. It came out of the tree in such a fury I almost lost it. I wasn't prepared for how heavy it would be hanging off the end of the long pole. It was like hooking some monstrous fish. Finally I got my hand around its legs and was able to drop the pole. I held it, upside down, high in the air. My trophy. The trophy, however, was a very agitated bird. It kept trying to break free. Its sharp, strong wings slapped me several times across the face—chicken shit flying everywhere, landing mostly on me.

Junior pulled out a handkerchief and wiped shit from my chin. "Good goin'!" he said slapping me on the back. I was laughing so hard I couldn't reply.

"You okay, Patrick?" he asked.

"That was crazy!" I managed.

We caught eleven chickens that night between the coop and the trees. I didn't attempt any more catches. I was happy with the one I got. Henry said if there were more out there they were probably too spooked to be caught that night.

We spent half an hour leaning against their pickup truck drinking a beer in celebration. Then I watched as they drove off down the driveway, feathers floating out the back of the truck.

As I walked to the house I thought about Henry and Junior. They were so different from the men I sometimes hung out with after work on Friday nights in a bar near my office. They were a congenial pair, communicating with each other using few words, I suppose, from working together for so many years.

Later that night I called Janet and related my chicken catching experience. She laughed and I could tell she was pleased that I had enjoyed myself. I told her about throwing the ball for Dolly and how Dolly was very used to taking rides in the truck. "I can't remember dad spending time with us like that," I said.

"Honestly, Patrick I think you're making way too much out of the dog."

I said good night without mentioning the envelope.

7

Early Friday morning Janet called to say she'd be delayed until noon. She had an appointment with a lawyer to discuss dad's estate. With the extra time Dolly and I took a new route on our morning walk. We followed the edge of the fields to the woods. In the shadows of trees we pushed through thick brush to the creek where I had often played as a child. I found a log in the shade and sat thinking about Charlie and Buddy. The creek was quite deep in the middle and we'd had many good times swimming there. I searched for the spot where we used to jump from a large tree. While holding a rope secured around a limb, we'd swing out over the water, then let go to drop into the cold water below. I couldn't locate the tree. Perhaps it was stupid of me to think that the tree would look the same after all these years. Or perhaps the tree was no longer there.

Dolly lay quietly by my side. Water gurgled peacefully as it rushed over stones rubbed smooth by countless years of flowing water. A heron landed at the edge of the creek. Its short stocky body gleamed blue-green in the sunlight. With stealth it waded in and stood staring as the water glided past its bright orange legs. Suddenly its head struck the water and came back up with a small fish in its beak.

It stretched out its neck and swallowed it whole. Dolly raised her head and the heron took off with a loud rasping 'skyew'.

After a few minutes a pair of wood ducks floated past. I hoped Dolly wouldn't move again. Wood ducks are notoriously shy and I knew any movement would scare them off. I hadn't seen wood ducks in years. They were beautiful birds, the green of their heads and rusty chest, set off by pronounced markings of white and black. I watched as they drifted by in peace.

I needed a notebook. There was so much to see and hear and I didn't want to forget it. I also decided that I would bring Janet here. She would enjoy seeing all the wild life and the woods alive with spring flowers.

I returned to the house and was working on the faucet in the upstairs bathroom when Janet arrived. Jobs were taking longer than they should, and daily I was adding more jobs to the list. Worse, I wasn't keeping up with editing my book. I had to start buckling down on my writing. Something was going to have to change, but I didn't see any help on the horizon. Janet was already doing a lot of work herself. And I was thankful she was taking care of all the paperwork involved.

I told Janet I was more than ready to take a break. Janet took egg salad sandwiches, brownies, and cool lemonade out to the porch where we ate in comfortable silence. When we were done eating I said, "I went through some of the photos while you were gone. Let me get the box."

"Take a look," I said when I returned. I started handing photos to her one at a time. "I thought you might want to keep this one."

"But Patrick, that's you with mom and me when you were a baby. Look how tiny you were. You should keep it."

"Take the original and I can get a copy later, but I'd like the one of mom and the watermelon, if you don't mind," I said showing it to her. It was a black and white photo. Mom was wearing a short-sleeved, print dress that gathered around the waist. She had on a large straw hat with her hair tucked beneath it.

"She had such a beautiful smile, didn't she? I actually remember that watermelon. She got a blue ribbon at the county fair for it. You keep it."

I showed her dad's fishing photo, the one of Aunt Edna, and some of the farm. "I don't really want these, and there are lots of photos of people I don't recognize with no names on the back." She slipped dad's photo over to be with the one of me as a baby.

"Well, put those in a pile and if I don't know them either we'll just throw them out."

"And then, there's this," I said pushing the envelope across the table. She looked at me expecting me to say more. When I didn't she opened it and pulled out the photo and paper. Looking at the back of the photo she could see 'baby Samuel' written on it in pencil.

"Is this you?" she asked, puzzled by the name.

I shook my head.

She unfolded the paper. I could see confusion on her face when she looked up at me and asked, "Who is this, Patrick?"

"According to that document," I said staring her in the eye, "that's our brother."

"What! How can that be? No one ever said anything about a brother," Janet said staring at the photo in disbelief. "Are you sure about that, Patrick?"

"Take a closer look at the document. Check the dates. Look at the names of the parents. How many Samuel and Ellen Crabtree's do you think there were, Janet?"

She studied the death certificate more carefully. "Death 1956. He died three years before I was born. What happened to him? He was what, just one year old?"

"Yes, about that. Read the cause of death." Her eyes searched the document again.

"Scarlet fever."

"I googled it last night. It was a prevalent disease back in the forties and fifties. One of many that children died from."

"Having children of my own, I can't even begin to imagine having one of them die. Our poor mom. That had to have been so hard. I'm stunned. Why weren't we told about this?"

"Part of our weird family, I guess."

"Patrick, just stop with that, okay. This is something we should have known."

"I agree. I've been thinking about it for the past few days trying to figure out why we didn't know. All I can come up with is back then people didn't handle death the way we do now, with the big productions at the funeral home and church. I think with babies they often buried them without any funeral at all—just the family at the grave site."

Janet eyed me as if I'd said something she didn't like.

"I'm not talking about our funeral for dad, Sis. But you know what I mean; lots of people now-a-days get carried away."

"Okay, say I agree with that. They still should have told us."

"Maybe it was just too painful for mom to talk about. Years ago when someone died it wasn't uncommon to never talk about the person again. Some people thought it was wrong to speak of the dead. Dead babies especially made people feel uncomfortable. Parents were supposed to put it behind them and deal with their grief in silence."

"That sounds awful. But…what happened to him?"

"The death certificate says scarlet fever."

"No, I mean, where's he buried? I've never seen his grave anywhere."

"Well, we never actually looked for one because up until now we never knew he existed. But I have an idea where to look."

"And where's that?" she asked looking at the child's photo again.

"I think he's buried in the same cemetery as mom and dad, but over in the older part. I've seen our Crabtree grandparents' headstones there while prowling around with Charlie and Buddy. I mean, think about it Janet. Both our parents were still alive; it would make sense that he was buried beside dad's parents, wouldn't it?"

"I guess it would, but honestly, I don't remember seeing their graves. Do you really think that's where he is?"

"Only one way to find out. Let's go take a look."

"You mean now?"

"Come on, Janet—do you want to know or not?"

"Okay. I guess I really am curious," she said getting up.

"Let's take the orchard truck. On the way back we can stop at the lumber yard. I need a sheet of plywood to fix the bathroom floor."

We parked by the cemetery gates which were closed, but not locked, and made our way on foot to mom and dad's graves. I was not eager to return there.

"I just want to say a little prayer," Janet said.

"Well, pray we can find Samuel."

"Patrick, really. If he's here we'll find him."

I led her to the far west corner. It was quite a few minutes before we located our grandparent's graves; everything in that part of the cemetery had become overgrown with neglected bushes.

"I never gave much thought about where our grandparents were buried," Janet said, looking at the headstones.

"Hard to feel much for people you've never met."

"My, haven't you gotten cynical over the years, Patrick."

"I've earned the right to be. Let's look around for Samuel's grave."

We walked around the area checking every headstone. Nothing. Finally Janet returned to our grandparent's graves. She pulled a big branch of spiarea away from grandpa's headstone so she could read it better. 'Albert Samuel Crabtree, 1878-1948' was barely visible.

I had been about to give up when Janet said, "Wait, Patrick. Look under this bush. I think there's another stone." Reaching in she said, "Yes, I can definitely feel something flat there, but I can't quite see the whole thing."

"I'll be right back," I said. "There's a pair of pruners in dad's truck."

I sprinted off to the truck and soon returned with the pruners. I began lopping off large spiraea branches until we could clearly see a small flat stone. "It's too dirty to read," Janet said leaning close.

I felt my hands shake as I pulled out a water bottle from my jacket pocket and began pouring water over the stone, the wet dirt muddying the knees of my jeans. Janet used her hands to wipe off the stone. Finally, letters began to emerge.

'Samuel Albert Crabtree. Age 1yr. 2 m.'

"I'll be damned," I said.

When we got back to the house it was nearly three o'clock. We worked for a while in silence, but neither of us was accomplishing much. We were both trying to wrap our heads around what we'd discovered. Now and then one of us would stop and make a comment.

"Do you think mom ever went to the cemetery to visit his grave?" Janet asked.

"I have no idea."

"I'd like to think she did, when no one else was around to disturb her. I know I would have."

Another time she said, "What do you think Sammy was like?"

"Sammy?"

"Yes, that's what I'm going to call him. He was just a year old after all."

Later I said what I had been thinking. "Now I know why I wasn't named Samuel, after dad."

I began telling Janet about a day when I was in grade school. I'd been wondering about my name. Charlie said he was named after his father. Buddy had said his real name was Theodore, though we better never call him that, after his grandfather. I'd never heard about anyone in my family named Patrick, so I asked Mom who I was named after. She told me that Crabtree was dad's last name, of course, and Olmstead was her name before she got married. But I still wanted to know where Patrick came from. She seemed hesitant to tell me. Finally she said Patrick was the name of a friend of dad's from the war. I asked if I'd ever met him and she said no. He had died. I didn't like having the name of a dead man. I pressured her with more questions, but she grew impatient. She told me terrible things happened in the war and I must promise to never ask dad about it. It was something he didn't want to talk about. She wouldn't say anymore. That was the end of finding out more about my name.

"Patrick Olmstead Crabtree. What a name," I said after finishing my story.

"I never knew that," Janet said.

"Well, it seems there's a lot we didn't know."

That night as I stood in front of the bathroom mirror getting ready to brush my teeth, I stopped and began examining my face. I wondered if Sammy would have looked anything like me, or perhaps more like Janet. I was slightly built and had light brown hair and blue eyes. Janet was darker, with dark brown hair and brown eyes, like dad. Janet was almost as tall as me. Dad was six feet tall. I was never going to pass five foot eight. We didn't look much like siblings, but we were as close as siblings could be.

Either way, I decided, it would have been nice having a big brother. Maybe I wouldn't have felt so alone.

8

It was Saturday, the beginning of the Memorial Day long weekend. There was no time for Dolly and me to go for a walk. Janet came early as the farmers said they would come around eight o'clock to get the cattle. When Janet arrived she informed me that George Schmidt, the auctioneer, was stopping by at two. It was obvious not much work was going to get done that day; not on the house and not on my book either. I'd barely touched my manuscript since the funeral. I was feeling a lot of anxiety over it, but felt unable to do anything more with everything else that was going on.

Janet handed me an envelope. She had stopped and picked up dad's mail on the way. "It's for you," she said.

Taking it I looked at the return address. It was from Nora's mother. I opened and read the condolence card and thoughtful message she'd written inside.

"She said she saw dad's obituary in the Muskegon Chronicle, and didn't know where I was living now, so she sent it to dad's address hoping I'd get it."

"That was really nice of her," Janet said. Then after moment she added, "Anything from Nora?"

"No, nothing." I laid the card on the counter and headed out to the barn to wait for the famers to arrive.

I stood studying the cows. I was going to miss them, even though I'd never milked these particular cows. The most contact I'd had with them was when I'd stop by the pasture and reached over the fence to rub my hand across a soft, wet nose, or watch as they grazed on clumps of grass. I always thought there was something peaceful about cows; the way they stood silently chewing their cud, or lay down in the shade of the large maple tree in the pasture twitching their tails to rid themselves of flies. They seemed so unhurried, so content.

So docile.

It took a while for the farmers to decide between them which cows each one would take. They only had trucks large enough to transport two cows at a time, which made it necessary for both farmers to make three trips. They lived on adjoining farms about ten miles from us, so it was nearly one o'clock by the time Ben came back for his last load.

I didn't expect that moving cows was going to be as entertaining as catching chickens, and it wasn't. But it did have its moments. The cows leaving in the first two loads boarded the trucks without complaint. Beautiful black and white Holsteins off to new homes, as if packing up and leaving was as common as heading out to the pasture for their daily nap. Ben soon found out, though, that there was a trouble-maker in the last group.

Of the two cows left, cow number one trotted up the ramp and onto the truck without incident. Cow number two had other plans. No way was she leaving home. She got as far as the ramp and balked. Ben had a rope around her neck.

Chapter 8

"Come on, Bossie. Time to go," he coaxed. She refused to move. The more he tugged, the deeper she dug her hooves into the ground.

"Get behind her and give her a push," Ben said to me.

He couldn't be serious, I thought. How was I going to convince something this big to move?

"She probably just needs a nudge," he added.

So I found myself at the wrong end of a Holstein that stood as tall as me, and weighed ten times more.

Ben pulled and I pushed.

"Come on, Patrick," Ben called. "Give it some more muscle."

I shoved harder.

Bossie took a step forward. Aha, success, I thought, and eased up a bit on my end—which was a huge mistake. It seemed Bossie had changed her mind. She stepped back, firmly planting one hind hoof on top of my right foot—all fifteen hundred pounds of her.

"She's on my foot!" I yelled up to Ben.

"Push!" he yelled back.

Then Bossie in her wisdom decided she'd had enough of this stupid man who was pushing her backside. She did the only thing she could do.

She raised her tail.

I saw what was coming but was trapped with Bossie on my foot. I leaned away as far as I could, missing most of what poured out the back end of that cow like a faucet suddenly turned on full blast.

I quickly learned cow shit was worse than chicken shit. For one thing, there's a lot more of it.

"Oh, my God! Get her off me!" I shouted.

Ben kept tugging and was now cursing, as well. Bossie turned her head back to look at me with triumph in her eyes. "Gotcha," those eyes seemed to say.

Just then I heard a loud bark. I felt Bossie tense up. Next came a series of barks, interspersed with growls. Dolly was not happy. Soon she was at Bossie's heels. With one quick jump, Bossie leapt on to the back of the truck.

Ben secured Bossie, then came down to take a look at me. He dissolved into laughter. I was a mess.

"Thanks a lot," I said.

"No problem, Patrick," he said slapping me on the back. Then looking at his hand, he wiped it off on his pants. "How's the foot?"

"I don't think anything's broken. Good thing the dirt here is pretty soft or it would've been crushed. I'll take a look at it when I get cleaned up."

"Well, I appreciate your help," he said shaking his head, then got into his truck and left. I could just imagine the local farmers getting together sharing their stories of me catching chickens and loading cows.

"Dolly, my hero," I said when she came up and started sniffing me. Only a dog could love the way I smelled. "You really are a farm dog."

I hosed myself off. Limping back to the house Janet asked, "What happened to you?"

"Don't ask," I replied as I headed for a shower, all the while revising my thoughts about cows being docile. By the time I was cleaned up, it was too late for lunch; the auctioneer was driving up to the house.

Two hours later, after George Schmidt had left, we finally settled down to a late lunch on the porch. While I was helping with the cattle, Janet had been taking things out to her car that she had boxed up to keep. She sat down next to me with a bag of mom's costume jewelry. She took out a necklace with a flower pendant hanging from it. "I think I'll let the girls go through these and pick out something of mom's, a memento of their grandmother. It's sad they never knew her. I'd have loved for them to have memories of mom."

"To be honest, Janet, I'm worried that I'm losing my memories of mom—my early memories anyway. They're overshadowed by the last years she lived. I was only twelve when she was diagnosed and seventeen when she died and it seems those five years are all I can remember. Then there was that terrible year I lived here alone with dad."

"There were good memories, too, Patrick. Try to think about those. You were definitely mom's favorite, being the baby of the family," she said with a smile. "You look more like her, too. I look like Dad." Janet continued to carry things to her car and I sat sipping a beer with my injured foot propped up on a chair, thinking about how things were after mom got sick.

For the first year mom was still able to do many things around the house, but before long the chemo started stealing her energy. Over time as she tried hard to keep doing the things she normally did but finally had to hand almost everything over to Janet and me. We shared cooking, dishes, laundry and cleaning, while still maintaining our school work. I also had to help dad with the chores.

Shortly after I turned fourteen things got even tougher. Janet had won a scholarship to Michigan State University. She wasn't going to accept it.

Mom and dad were at odds. Mom wouldn't hear of Janet giving up the scholarship; dad insisted she was needed at home. But mom wouldn't give in. She rarely argued with dad, but on this topic she was adamant. She said Janet had worked hard—had been valedictorian—and this was her reward. We'd find a way to manage.

So that fall Janet left for college and I was in charge of most everything. Dad gave me a break from the chores during the week, but on weekends I still had to help with the milking.

But plans often change and a year later Janet returned home and announced she was dropping out of school to marry Phil. He was going to go to medical school and she was going to work to support them until he finished. Mom was upset and had long talks with her about marriage, but the decision was ultimately Janet's. Mom attended the wedding in a wheelchair, but didn't stay for the reception. She was far too weak for that.

Janet came back from her car. "My car's full. I'm not sure what I'm going to do with all this stuff. Aren't there some things you want, Patrick?"

"I can't think of anything at the moment. Are you heading off then?"

"Yeah. I'll see you in the morning. Have a good night and take care of your foot."

"I will," I said. I had every intention of working on my book that evening. I tried for over an hour, but couldn't keep my mind from drifting off to other things. Finally I gave up, went outside and built a campfire where dad used to burn things near the shed. I gathered dead limbs from the yard and orchard. Soon I had a nice warm fire going. I grabbed an old lawn chair from the porch and turned a log on end so I could prop up my foot. It was a beautiful evening as Dolly and I settled down next to flickering flames. There had always been something peaceful about a campfire.

9

Sunday morning. The rain came down in a continuous drizzle; the wind cold and fierce. Dolly and I would miss our walk that day, though honestly I doubted my foot was up to going very far. I was especially tired that morning. I hadn't slept well worrying about all that still needed to be done. My plan had been to start getting the lawn in shape, but that wasn't going to happen either. After breakfast I decided to go out to the shed and see if I could at least get the lawn mower going.

While Dolly lay inside the doorway watching it rain, I worked on the mower. After an hour I knew it was hopeless. I threw down the wrench in exasperation. It wasn't just the lawn mower that upset me. I was angry dad had let so many things go around the house and farm. It left me to play the role of hired hand once again. A role I hated.

I decided not to waste any more of my time. I'd have to go to town and buy a new lawn mower. It was frustrating. I didn't have time for these problems.

All I could do was wait. When the rain stopped and everything dried out, I'd have to hook the tractor up to the hay mower and go over the tall grass and weeds. After that I'd rake it. Then I'd still need to go over it again with the new lawn mower to get rid of all the stubble. It would probably take up most of a day. I hoped my foot would feel better by then, because at that moment it ached and hurt with every step.

The auction was set for next Saturday and all the machinery was going to be sold. This meant the job had to be finished in the next few days. We planned on setting some of the furniture out in the yard to be auctioned and Janet was getting a sign to put out front saying the house was for sale by owner. We'd probably end up having to get a realtor. But who knows? Lots of people show up at auctions.

Giving up on the mower I returned to the house to pick a different job. But first I rummaged through the medicine cabinet in the bathroom for some Tylenol to stop the throbbing in my foot.

I was just pouring myself a cup of coffee to warm up when my phone rang. It was my boss, Jack. I doubted I was going to like the call, so I decided not to answer. Instead I finished my coffee with my foot propped up, letting the Tylenol do its job. Finally, I braced myself and called him back. We made small talk for a couple minutes, then he got down to business. It was just as I'd thought.

"Patrick, the reason I'm calling is I'm at the office this morning trying to catch up on paperwork. I could really use you here. We're swamped." His tone was friendly, but I knew him well enough to pick up the underlying current of agitation.

"And next week Brian's vacation is going to start. I'd ask him to delay it, but he's already bought tickets for Disney World. You know he only gets his kids once a month. I hate putting pressure on you like this, but we're going to be two people short. Is there any way you could come back to work sooner?"

I doubted he felt too badly about putting pressure on me. I sighed. Did he honestly think I was just taking it easy, having myself a nice little vacation of my own? I liked Jack, but there was no way I would leave Janet to finish all this alone.

"I just can't, Jack. I can't leave this all on my sister's shoulders. There's a ton of work left to do here. We're having a farm auction in a week and are trying to get the house ready to sell. I'm going to need every day of my time off. I wish I could come back sooner, and I will if I can, but I can't make any promises."

Not surprisingly he was rather put out by my answer; his tone no longer friendly, he ended the call abruptly. Things were probably going to be a bit chilly between us when I returned.

I put on another pot of coffee for Janet who was running late, then got out a bag of cookies. I decided I better quickly check my email, and then I'd have to get to work on something.

Since there was no internet at dad's house I'd been forced to set up temporary dial-up service through his phone line. I hated using it, but I had to have access to my email. It seemed especially slow that morning. After a couple minutes of irritating squawks from the computer I was nearly at the end of my patience. Finally, I got into my email. It certainly did nothing to improve my mood.

It seemed I was disappointing a lot of people that morning.

I had a message from my editor, Stan. He was upset he hadn't heard from me. He'd informed me a while back that he wanted me to do a rewrite of chapter three, which I'd already done once. It was a pivotal chapter in my book and he said it still needed work. The dialog was still too stiff. And I needed to work on the budding romance between my main character and the woman he'd met at the art show.

Make it more believable. He thought I should reveal more about this woman. Show the readers what it was that had drawn him to her.

I hadn't even started working on it yet.

I wondered if the day could get any more stressful as I picked up the phone and reluctantly dialed another person who was already upset with me.

He picked up on the second ring. "Stan, its Patrick---"

"Where've you been?" he demanded cutting me off. He had a booming voice loud enough to be heard across the room. I held the phone away from my ear as he continued.

"I know you told me about your dad and going to where ever it is you used to live and all, but you told me you'd stay in touch."

I was sick and tired of people being angry with me. I was stretched thin trying to cope with all the demands other people had placed on my life. But I would have to tread lightly. I knew Stan had a short fuse.

"I'm sorry Stan, but it's been crazy here. You have no idea. Have you ever been stepped on by a cow? You should see my foot. How about catching chickens in trees, or setting up for an auction? Now there's a project for you. I could write quite a book about that by itself." I was trying to lighten the mood, but that worked about as well as me getting the lawnmower going.

"Well, leave that for some other day, Patrick," he said clearly not amused by my defense. "We have work to get done on this book if you intend on getting it published."

"I do, Stan. I'm sorry I've gotten so far behind." I made a decision then. "Tomorrow is Memorial Day. I'll take the day off from work around here and spend the entire day doing nothing but the rewrite of chapter three and get it off to you."

"Well, I hope so. I'm not trying to be difficult, Patrick," he said his voice softening a bit. "I know things got dumped on you. But I really need this."

"I promise. Tomorrow it will be done."

Hanging up I hoped I could pull it off.

I had returned to the kitchen table with my coffee and pad of paper filled with jobs to do when Janet finally arrived. It was a little after ten. All I really felt like doing at that moment was getting in my car and heading back to Chicago. I didn't think I had the energy or the patience to continue with the pile of work staring at me.

She filled her coffee mug and put in two spoons of sugar. Stirring it she said, "Sorry about being late. I was helping Mary Beth with a few things." Then, seeing the look on my face she added, "I was just trying to help out a bit. After all I've been spending a lot of time there."

"No problem," I said.

"How's the foot?" she asked sitting down.

"Not great."

She helped herself to a couple cookies. Reaching over she gave one to Dolly who had positioned herself next to her in anticipation, eyes focused on the treat. She gulped it down in one bite, then looked up hoping there'd be more. There was.

"She shouldn't be eating all that junk," I said, but Janet ignored me.

"Well, tomorrow you can give your foot a rest. I'm supposed to invite you for a barbecue for Memorial Day. I'm staying over tonight and Phil and the girls are driving out in the morning. They've got the pool up and running, so if the weather's good we should be able to have a relaxing day for a change. And Mary Beth already has a ton of food made. That's what I was helping her with."

She had to be kidding, right? Tomorrow? The day I was supposed to work on my book? The day I was supposed to get Stan off my back?

And besides that, her breezy attitude was getting to me. I was glad to hear she thought she could take some time off. Getting in the car and leaving sounded better all the time.

I let out a sigh of frustration.

"I'm sorry, Sis, I wish I could, but I just can't. I planned on spending the entire day working on my book. I've gotten way behind."

"You could come for a couple hours, at least. Mary Beth would love to have you. It would be good for you to get away for a bit."

"Why does everyone seem to think they know how I should spend my time?" I said, my voice beginning to raise in exasperation. Did I not have a life of my own anymore?

"Patrick—"

"Look, I told you. I can't. My editor sent me a long list of corrections I need to make. I'm on a tight time line—I can't keep putting it off."

I picked up my pad of jobs and started studying it.

"Geez, Patrick, I was only suggesting a couple hours."

"You're not listening to me!" I shouted slamming the pad down on the counter. "Don't you get it? I don't have an extra couple of hours! My days are filled with making repairs and by night I'm so exhausted I fall asleep in the chair. Nothing's getting done. Not here. And not on my book either."

I got up and stood down hard on my foot sending a shooting pain up my leg.

"This isn't some kind of hobby I'm talking about," I continued no longer trying to keep my temper under control. "I have a contract. I can't screw it up. Being a writer, getting a book published, it's all I've ever wanted—but no one seems to get that. Not dad. Not Nora. And apparently, not you either!"

Janet became very quiet. If she was shocked by my outburst she didn't show it. When she did speak every word was measured.

"Well, you listen to me, Patrick. I'm sick of you always feeling sorry for yourself. It's always someone else's fault that you haven't written the great American novel by now. Maybe you think you should've won the Pulitzer Prize already. I don't know."

Then losing control herself she added, "But let me tell you this. Everything is not about you. You're not the only one who didn't get what they wanted out of life. I'm not sure if anyone does. But definitely not me either!

With that she pitched her cup in the sink and stormed out of the house letting the screen door slam behind her. I went to the door and called after her, but she didn't even turn around. I watched as she walked down the lane, her shoulders hunched against the pouring rain.

I returned to the table and sat there shaking. Dolly came over and put her head in my lap. "It's okay, Dolly," I said as I stroked her head and looked into her soft brown eyes. "It's okay."

I felt horrible. The last person I wanted to fight with was Janet. We were both overwhelmed. None of this was her fault.

When she didn't come back after a few minutes I got up and went to the downstairs bathroom where I began pulling up loose tiles.

I might as well see what damage I could do there while I waited.

About fifteen minutes later I heard Janet come in and move around the kitchen. Then she appeared in the doorway of the bathroom, wiping her hair with a towel.

"I'm sorry, Patrick."

"Me, too," I said, putting down the tools I was using. "We're both over tired. The amount of work to get done here is taking a toll on both of us."

"It's more than that, Patrick. Things have been hard at home with me being gone so much. I'm not getting a lot of sleep and… well, the truth is, Phil and I are having problems."

I looked up at her tear-streaked face.

"What kind of problems?"

"I'm pretty sure Phil is seeing someone else, especially now that I can be counted on to be gone every weekend."

"That bastard—"

She held up her hand. "I can't talk about it right now, Patrick. I shouldn't have taken it out on you. It's not your fault. And I'm sorry for not listening. I do know how much your writing means to you. You do what's best for you."

Later that night I sat in dad's recliner with a beer listening to the rain beating down on the roof. I thought about what Janet had said. It was true. For years I'd only thought about my own disappointments. I hadn't given any thought to what Janet had always wanted.

The life Janet lived was far from her childhood dreams. It had always bothered me that she dropped out of college to marry Phil. Honestly, I couldn't stand the guy. He always had this condescending manner when he talked to her. That she had quit college to support their family and given up her life's ambition of becoming a biologist had never set well with me. Once Phil got his degree, she was supposed to go back to college; but then the kids came along, time passed, and it never happened.

She had always excelled at school, especially in science. Even during the summer she read constantly. Not the romance novels her friends were so fond of; Janet read serious stuff. She would come back from the library every week with stacks of books usually reserved for adults. Her bedroom was wallpapered with posters. Covering every space were endangered animals, birds, butterflies, insects and plants. She had become very adept at identifying the things of nature.

I remembered one book in particular, Silent Spring by Rachel Carson, had made an enduring impression on her. She had checked it out of the library several times. Its description of the effects of pesticides on the environment helped launch the environmental movement, and Janet was determined to do what she could to change things. The fact our father sprayed so many chemicals was not lost on her.

Janet tried to talk to dad about what she'd learned from her reading one evening as we sat out on the porch, Silent Spring open on her lap. I thought she was being very brave. When she started we all knew it wasn't going to end well. It didn't take long before dad had gotten angry and told her in no uncertain terms that she didn't know what she was talking about; that she was to keep that rubbish out of the house. After that Janet learned to keep Silent Spring, and many of her other books as well, out of dad's sight.

I sat there still thinking about the book and the Saturday Janet had come home from the library, flushed and a bit winded from the three mile ride on her bicycle. I was in the kitchen with mom, holding a glass of milk and eating chocolate chip cookies fresh out of the oven. It was obvious Janet was excited about something and couldn't wait to tell us.

"Well, what are you so happy about, Janet?" Mom inquired as she popped another pan of cookies into the oven. I was busy helping myself to more cookies. There was no end to how many I could eat.

After setting her book bag on the kitchen counter and getting a glass of milk and cookies of her own, she said, "Wait until you hear this. You know what a stickler Mrs. Shriver is."

Mom nodded. The regimental running of the library by Mrs. Shriver was not up for question. She'd been there so long she was the only librarian we could remember. Most students I knew did their best to avoid her. I usually let one of the assistants check out my books. Mrs. Shriver was never one to be overly friendly with students; but Janet had never seemed intimidated by her.

"Well, when I gave her the books I was returning today," Janet continued, "she noticed I had "Silent Spring" again. She said they'd had that book since 1962, and no one checked it out anymore but me. Then she reached over and placed a stamp and an ink pad in front of the book and opened the cover. After stamping something inside, she handed the book back to me."

Janet reached into her bag and pulled out Silent Spring. When she opened the cover to show us, we could clearly see red block letters announcing the book had been 'DISCARDED'.

"You mean it's yours?" Mom asked as I reached over and took another cookie.

"Yup. It's mine to keep, but Mrs. Shriver said we should keep that a secret between the two of us."

"That was really nice of her, Janet. I hope you remembered to thank her," Then smiling at me, Mom snatched the cookie from my hand and ate it.

Sitting there thinking about Janet, I wondered if she still had the book. If Janet was right about Phil, I hoped she divorced the son-of-a-bitch, took her half of the money from dad's estate, and did something with her life that she wanted to do for a change.

10

Monday morning and the rain still hadn't stopped. The temperature hovered around sixty degrees. Water dripped off the trees, and formed puddles in the driveway. A steady stream of water traveled down the roof and flowed off the eaves, making a muddy, soggy mess of the yard. It was definitely not a good day for a Memorial Day party. I wondered if Janet had stayed at Mary Beth's over night or gone home. I tried to call her, but got no answer.

While the coffee brewed I put out food and water for Dolly. Then I put my laptop and my papers and pens on the kitchen table, opened the windows so I could hear the rain, and started on my manuscript.

Dolly lay most of the morning stretched out on her side sleeping in front of the screen door. The sounds of Dolly's snoring and the soft drumming of the rain made for a calming effect. For hours I wrote and rewrote. Words just fell into place. It had been a long time since I'd had a writing day like that. It felt good. I thought about what Janet had said, that I should do what was best for me. I felt I'd finally gotten permission to be myself; to not have to apologize for my writing any longer.

At three o'clock, after reading the chapter through one last time, I finally hit the 'send' button. It was on its way to Stan.

I realized I was hungry. I'd skipped breakfast that morning in my hurry to get started. After sitting for so long my back ached, so I made a sandwich and began eating it as I wandered around the house.

Some things were getting done at least. In the kitchen Janet had emptied the cupboards, leaving me just enough dishes to cook for myself, but the cupboards still needed painting. I didn't see how I was going to get that done. Maybe a really good scrubbing would suffice. The downstairs bathroom was finished, the plumbing fixed and the floor repaired. Not a half-bad job I told myself.

In the small living room-dining room it was as dark as usual. The heavy brocade drapes didn't allow for much light. I flicked on the overhead light switch and stared at the drab wallpaper. It must have been fifty years old. It was faded and dirty. I was willing to bet this would be one of the first things to go when the new owner moved in. What a job that would be.

Janet had taken out all the dishes and knick-knacks from the china hutch, including mom's collection of salt and pepper shakers, and boxed them up. Seeing the empty spaces where mom had kept her assortment of little treasures saddened me. Even twenty seven years later when I stopped to look at them, I'd always felt her presence. Now her space had been emptied and she was no longer there.

I walked over to look at the bookshelf behind the chair where mom had always sat. Like Janet, Mom read a lot, getting most of her books from the library; but a few books of her own lined the dusty shelves. Two books on gardening and a fat book of quilting ideas were placed side by side. Several cookbooks, well-worn from use, had slips of paper sticking out marking some of her favorite recipes. Next to them, two old Zane Grey mystery novels looked interesting. I pulled one out and opened it. Inside someone had written with a fountain pen, 'Peter Olmstead'. I recognized that as my grandfather's name. I set both books aside and took out another one. It was a book of American poetry. Mom's name was written inside in her neat handwriting. I decided I'd like to keep that book, as well. I took the three books and placed them beside my computer on the table.

Ditching my coffee mug I grabbed a Coke from the refrigerator and headed upstairs. That bathroom, too, was finished. Janet's old bedroom had been emptied of everything personal; all that was left was furniture. But as I entered dad's room I saw that she'd never come back to finish her work there. I decided then it was something we needed to do together.

I turned and stared at the door to my old bedroom. Janet had made it clear; cleaning out that room was up to me. It might seem strange, but until then I had tried not to look too much at my old room, even though I'd slept there every night since the funeral. I was afraid if I did I would be pulled back to a time I didn't want to remember. Each morning I'd grabbed my clothes out of my duffle bag, closed the bedroom door, and gone to take a shower. At night I returned with Dolly and fell into bed exhausted. Sometimes I never even turned on the light. Going into that room was like entering a time warp, but I knew I couldn't avoid it any longer.

I opened the door and entered my past.

I sat on my bed and tried to take it all in. It looked the same as it did when I'd left in anger and desperation over twenty years ago. Until my return it had been closed up like a tomb. On the bed a colorful quilt made by my mother nearly brought tears to my eyes as I thought about how much I missed her. The design of red, white and blue squares and triangles had always reminded me of a huge flag. Rubbing my hand over the quilt I realized I'd never really appreciated how much time it must have taken her to sew it. She'd made a quilt for Janet as well; something in a flower pattern if I remembered correctly. Making our quilts seemed such an act of love.

Posters of Pink Floyd, Van Halen, and The Rolling Stones were still tacked on the pale blue walls. I'd always liked to play my music loud. Really loud. Much to my parent's discomfort. My music could rattle windows.

Strewn across the desk were papers, pens, books and folders. Off to the side a reading lamp, its shade a silhouette of ducks, was covered with dust. Turning it on only emphasized how dirty the room had gotten. I opened a folder on top of the desk. It was a story I'd started to write the night before I left. I'd closed it and moved on.

I began opening bureau drawers. Old underwear and t-shirts in one; still more t-shirts in another. The bottom drawer held a couple pair of jeans. I pulled out a pair and held them up. Was I really that skinny back then? I'd put on a few pounds and even if I wanted to, I'd never be able to wear those again.

The closet was miniscule compared to the one in my apartment. A few long-sleeved shirts hung next to my only pair of dress pants, the legs lined with shiny creases from too much ironing. I saw my favorite old denim jacket with frayed cuffs and was reminded of the many times I'd worn it on cool nights at football games. I could no longer wear that either. On the floor a pair of black, scuffed dress shoes sat next to a well-worn pair of gym shoes. To the side, my beat-up red backpack with the broken zipper was right where I'd left it. Everything smelled musty and made me sneeze, so I closed the doors.

Chapter 10

Once again I found myself back at my desk. Memories washed over me of the hours I'd spent sitting there. That was where I'd done my homework. That was the place I'd first begun to write. Pulling up a chair I sat down and opened the bottom drawer. It held several folders full of papers.

Over the next two hours I read them all.

Like all teenagers I wanted to fit in, so when Buddy and Charlie tried out for the junior varsity football team, I signed up for tryouts, too. It seemed ridiculous considering my size. Charlie and Buddy were big boys—I, on the other hand, looked more like a twelve year old. What was even more incredible was that I'd made the team. No one seemed terribly shocked by that. Considering the size of my school what they'd really been looking for was enough warm bodies to make up a team.

I dreaded every practice. For six weeks I was tossed around as if I were the football. I was punched, knocked over, thrown on the ground, had the wind knocked out of me, and made the target of crude remarks about my size and my inability to play the game. Every afternoon I headed home with a new set of bruises and more pain than I wanted to admit. Even with my strength from working on the farm, I was no match for anyone. Buddy and Charlie gave me as much leeway as they could, but there were guys on the team who got a thrill out of seeing me fly through the air. One of them was Mason Getz—better known as 'The Tank'.

The Tank was bigger than me in every direction. He outweighed me by at least a hundred pounds. When I stood in front of him I stared at his chest. Just the sight of him made me want to run for the locker room. No one got by The Tank—not from our team, and not from any other team. He was just unstoppable. If he took aim at you, the best you could hope for was there'd be a lot of people who showed up at your funeral.

One afternoon The Tank came out of the locker room late. We were already paired up practicing our ball toss; when The Tank realized he needed a partner he ambled up to Buddy who had been tossing the ball with me and pushed him aside. "Let me see what you've got, Midget," he shouted at me. I had the ball in my hand so I threw him my best pass. Just then the coach's whistle blew as he called out for us to change to tackling practice. Before I could even start any evasive moves, The Tank put his hands around my waist, hiked me over his head, and slammed me to the ground.

I felt something give near my shoulder, followed by a sharp pain. Coach was summoned and soon the entire team stood around looking at me writhing on the ground in agony. I was taken to emergency where my parents were called. My mother came and was near hysterical when she saw me—I had to work hard to get her calmed down, rather than the other way around. Maybe it was her having lost little Samuel that made her so upset seeing me hurt, though I couldn't have known that then, or maybe it was that she had already been diagnosed with cancer. Whatever it was, she couldn't stop crying.

I had x-rays and it was determined that I'd broken my collar bone, but it would heal eventually. For now, I was sentenced to sit on the bench at practice and at games. I did that for a couple weeks, and then I just stopped showing up. No one seemed to notice.

I've always credited becoming a writer to having broken my collar bone. With the extra time I had because I couldn't help dad with the chores—which he grumbled about constantly telling me football was a waste of time—I was becoming bored. Lying in bed one night reading a Super Man comic that I'd almost memorized, I wondered if I could make a comic of my own—with the little boxes, pictures and a story. I, of course, would be the super hero. But first I'd need a name. I decided to call myself Mega Man, alter ego of Patrick Crabtree. Of course, I drew Mega Man larger than all the other characters.

I spent a couple hours making boxes, drawing some rudimentary pictures, and putting in the speech bubbles to tell my story. It was a pretty dumb story and crude looking, but when I took it to school and shared it with Buddy and Charlie, they thought it was pretty funny—especially the way I'd drawn myself.

Maybe I was on to something.

For weeks I drew comics. I started adding Buddy and Charlie as my good-guy sidekicks. Together we defended people being attacked by thugs, stopped school bullies from stealing lunches from the little kids, helped the police find a suspected murderer, and got back stolen bank money. The kids at school loved them and wanted me to include them in my comics. But I soon grew tired of drawing all those boxes and the pictures to go in them. Drawing wasn't something I liked or excelled at. Besides, I found the boxes too confining. I had a lot more I wanted to say. So I began writing stories instead. This allowed for Buddy, Charlie, and me to have a lot more interesting adventures.

One day after showing Buddy and Charlie my latest story, Charlie said to me, "How come we're always the sidekicks? Why can't we be the heroes sometimes?" He realized that Mega Man was getting better roles and more of the action. They began lobbing me with so many ideas that I started carrying around a little notebook to write them all down. Finally, I told them to stop. I would write an adventure for each of them making them the hero. But after that, I was retiring from writing stories about friends.

A month later I gave them each their own special story placed in a notebook with a drawing on the front portraying them as the main character in action. I had thought hard about the kind of hero they might like to be. I'd made myself a crime fighter, but there were other types of heroes.

Buddy loved everything about outer space. He read science fiction, kept track of the NASA space launches, and knew the names of all the astronauts. In his story Buddy built a spaceship in his parent's garage. Charlie and I were there to help. We painted the spaceship red with silver trim and USA in large black letters on the sides.

When the spaceship was finished we encountered a problem. It was too big to go out the door. But his parents were so proud of him that his dad helped take off the garage door and made the opening big enough to pull the spaceship out and set it up in their driveway. Soon the whole neighborhood was there anticipating the launch, with Buddy at the controls, Charlie as co-pilot, and me as navigator. Our families stood in Buddy's front yard waving and wiping tears from their eyes, and our teachers and all the school kids lined the street, as we blasted off into space.

Charlie's story was a little more difficult. Finally I remembered how he loved speed. The faster he went the better. He rode his bicycle like a maniac. Charlie became a race car driver. He entered the Indy 500 driving a sleek yellow race car with the number 3 on the side, to represent the three of us. Buddy and I made up the pit crew. Of course, Charlie won. His picture on the front cover showed him taking the victory lap holding the checkered flag.

It was all in good fun. The stories just seemed to fly off my fingertips. Buddy, Charlie, and I were inseparable.

Though I was no longer writing stories for friends, I continued writing by working on the school newspaper, the Brooks Creek High School Spirit, and was the editor my junior and senior years. Now and then I'd slip in a cartoon or two; I was only censored by my supervisor a couple of times. I always tried to include the names of as many students as I could because I knew people liked to see their names in print. I especially liked covering the football games, now that I was no longer on the team getting beaten up. Charlie was team captain by then, but Buddy, who actually disliked playing football, was at my side with his camera. It was fun to go back to my bedroom afterwards and write up the articles from my notes. Those years solidified in me what I wanted to do when I got out of high school.

I wanted to become a journalist.

When I finished reading I sat back in my chair. I could see that even at a young age I'd had a good imagination and a way with words. I liked to think I still did. But the enthusiasm for writing I had back then didn't exist for me anymore. Writing my book had simply been work. I wanted that feeling back. I just wasn't sure how to get it.

11

The next morning I woke to the sun shining through the dirty bedroom window. I pushed back the covers and got up, almost tripping over Dolly still asleep on the floor next to the bed. I'd had a restless night dreaming of spaceships, football games, and my mother, all mysteriously mixed together. Dolly had finally given up. Tired of my tossing and turning, she had moved to the floor to sleep.

I showered and inspected my foot. It was a deep purple, but didn't hurt that much anymore. After dressing I headed downstairs and made coffee. As it was brewing I made a decision. I returned to my bedroom where I retrieved the old backpack from the closet and dumped the contents onto the floor. An algebra textbook, some history papers, a couple Snickers bars—hard as rocks, and an empty potato chip bag spilled out at my feet. I picked up a note from Buddy that said, "You look like a space alien with your new haircut." I smiled at the memory. It was a pretty bad haircut.

I took the empty backpack over to my desk and pulled out a notebook from the top drawer. After I ripped out the used pages, I put it in my backpack and went back downstairs. There I added a thermos of coffee, some pens, and Dolly's rawhide chewy. As an afterthought, I added mom's American poetry book. Soon the two of us were on our way back to the creek.

As we reached the bank something quickly scurried beneath a bush. From the glimpse I caught of it I thought it was a fox. Dolly took off after it. I called and called but she kept going, following whatever it was into the bushes. I walked closer to the creek and saw muddy dog-like tracks near the water. We must have interrupted a fox getting a drink. I wondered if that's what killed the last chicken we never apprehended. A few days after Henry and Junior snared the others, I'd found feathers and bones in a pile behind the barn.

I went to the log and placed the backpack next to it and sat for a while waiting for Dolly's return. She came back panting; her belly covered with thick mud from crawling under the bushes and her fur full of burrs. She waded belly-deep into the cool water, lapping as she went. Finally she raised her head and stood, water dripping from her muzzle, watching a school of minnows circle her legs.

"Let's walk down the creek a bit, Dolly, if you're not too tired," I laughed. We made our way along the bank. It was difficult going as we forged through thick brush. We often had to step into the water to make our way around. I carried my shoes and tried to be careful of my injured foot while I headed for the sharp bend in the creek that I remembered.

We stopped for a few minutes and watched some crayfish gathered near the bank in a pile of rocks. I heard a call of an eagle, and though I searched the trees, I couldn't find it. A black snake sliced through the water and hid under a log, wanting to avoid whatever had disturbed it.

Once we reached the bend I saw a large tree had fallen across the creek blocking our way. It was disappointing, but it would be impossible to continue unless we went through the thick brush, up a steep embankment, then down the other side.

There was a time I knew every curve of the creek. If I kept going, in about three miles I'd meet up with the Muskegon River. Buddy, Charlie and I canoed this water one summer when we were fifteen and the water level was still high from the spring thaw. We borrowed a canoe from Buddy's grandfather and headed out one warm day with some sandwiches and a six-pack of coke, which we tied to the canoe and hung over the side to keep cool. We looked forward to a pleasant drift down the creek.

Things didn't go as planned. It seemed every forty to sixty feet we had to stop, get out of the canoe, and portage around brush and logs and other debris in the water. We did more carrying the canoe than riding in it. Honestly, we probably could have walked the three miles faster.

For a few minutes I watched a pair of mallards and their seven ducklings swim near the toppled tree, the soft ripples from their paddling slowly radiating to the bank. I decided it was time to go back. The mosquitoes were relentless. I'd have to add repellant to my backpack.

Back at the log I gave Dolly her chewy and poured myself some coffee. Pulling out the notebook I began making notes about the things I'd encountered at the creek. I wrote about the mallards and crayfish, then the heron and wood ducks from a few days ago. I added notes about hearing the eagle and other sounds and smells, the rustling of the wind through the upper branches of the aspens, the dripping of the dew making little plopping sounds when the drops hit the water, the creaking sound the large trees made as they swayed in the breeze, the overpowering scent of pine, and the pungent smell of last fall's dead leaves that had piled up in the water along the bank.

I jotted down a few notes about the canoe trip for later, then looking around I saw that Dolly had gotten up and was investigating something. *Dolly has found a frog. She doesn't know quite what to do with it, so for now she's just following it until she decides.*

The notebook was divided by three pocket folders. I flipped to a new section and wrote "MOM" at the top. I began listing memories I had of her:

When I was eight years old I had my tonsils out. Mom made an exception about not spoiling her children. She bought every flavor of Popsicle for me, and so as not to let Janet feel left out, she bought the same for her.

One time when mom came to a parent meeting at school she was wearing a pretty pink and blue flowered dress with a full skirt. Her long hair, which was normally worn up, was curled around her shoulders, and she even had on a touch of lipstick. I thought she was the most beautiful mother there.

When I showed mom my cartoons, she thought they were funny.

I checked the time. It was after ten. I needed to get back and start working. I decided that I was going to wait a day on the lawn, let the grass dry out, and repair and paint the porch steps instead. Janet insisted that I paint the screen door as well. I thought about objecting, but I was afraid she might decide to add painting the whole porch if I did. "It's all about curb appeal," she had said.

On the way back to the house I realized I felt better than I had in a long time. The exercise and work were clearly good for me. I'd lost a few pounds and had more energy. There was this feeling nibbling around the edges of my being that almost felt like peace but I'd learned a long time ago to be wary of trusting my feelings too much. Change could happen fast.

Chapter 11

By the time I reached the house my feet were soaked. I had another pair of shoes, but needed some dry socks. I'd need to do laundry soon. I wondered if there were any socks in one of dad's drawers. I went upstairs to his room and began searching through drawers and soon found plenty of socks. Unfortunately they hadn't been mated. I began laying them on top of the dresser until I had a pair. One or two more pair should do me until I could wash my clothes. I reached down to the bottom to get another possible mate when I felt something. It was thick and smooth and felt like paper. I pulled it out.

I opened the copy of Chicago Magazine, the one I'd sent dad, to my article still marked with the yellow sticky note. He hadn't thrown it away after all.

But why had he kept it in a sock drawer— as if he was hiding it for some reason? It struck me as odd, but there was a lot about dad that often didn't make sense to me. The realization, though, that he had kept it pleased me. Still, I wished I knew what he'd thought of it.

That night after I'd done my dishes I spent some time going through the rest of the photos. I pulled out a few more for Janet and stuck them in an envelope. The others weren't of much interest. They were mostly photos of other people's lives and had nothing to do with me or Janet. Soon I'd try to get to the box of letters.

As I sat by the campfire that evening I watched the sunset of blue, orange, and purple clouds fill the sky as the sun dropped behind the barn. The orchard trees were in silhouette and I clearly saw little green apples, the size of marbles, glistening in a cover of dew on some of the lower branches. I was glad there would be at least a few apples.

The orchard surrounded the farm buildings on three sides. It made the whole farm feel cozy. The trees offered a beautiful view in every season. White and pink blossoms in the spring, green leaves and shiny red apples in the summer and fall, and branches with snow and ice that often sparkled in the sun during the coldest parts of winter.

I got up and went into the house and returned with my notebook. I wrote for a long time by the light of the campfire. It was remarkable how different the farm looked to me. I was able to see it without looking through the lens of my father, which had clouded everything for me with sadness and anger. It reminded me of putting together a puzzle. I knew from the cover what the picture was supposed to look like, but as I fit the pieces of the farm together, I realized it didn't look at all like the picture on the box. It was better.

I lay in bed that night with Dolly beside me listening to her sigh as she settled down into sleep. I stroked her head and began thinking what great company she was and struggled with what to do with her when it was time for me to go back to Chicago. I didn't want to give her up. But an apartment was no place for Dolly.

I dreaded going back to Chicago, not just to a job I hated, but to my dreary apartment. When I moved into the apartment it had not been a big deal. I thought it was temporary until I found a better place. But I'd never really looked for anything else once I settled in. The rent wasn't horrible, at least not for Chicago. The size was convenient—one bedroom, a kitchen-dining room combo, small living room and one bath. No lawn to mow. No big upkeep. Laundry room three flights down. What more did I need? Well, maybe a view would have been nice. The only windows I had looked out at the brick wall of the apartment building across from me. But, like I said, it was temporary—for years now. Somehow I had let myself get into a depressing rut.

I thought about the posters hanging on the walls of my bedroom at the farm. The walls of my apartment were still the same blank white walls that were there the day I moved in. I needed to do something about that. I had a minimum of furniture bought from a discount store. A dinette set was my office/writing area. I ate my meals in front of the TV. Usually fast food or something I microwaved. I thought about the porch and how much I was going to miss eating my meals there.

Then there was the parking issue. It was a Chicago nightmare.

The opportunity to exercise was difficult. I'd thought about getting a bicycle as some of the people in other apartments had done, but I didn't relish carrying one up and down all those flights of stairs. In order to not have to ride in congested areas, I'd have to get a bike rack on my car and drive somewhere. I knew I could never convince myself to do it.

A gym membership was out of the question. Just the thought of donning gym clothes and working out next to guys with bulging muscles made me think too much of walking out onto the football field when I was fourteen. I liked the way I looked now. I didn't want to return to the heavier version of me. I'd have to come up with some way to keep that from happening.

I rolled onto my side, still awake after hours without sleep. I listened as owls out in the orchard called to each other. There were excited sounds from millions of insects chirruping, whirring, and buzzing in the dark.

Back in Chicago I knew I'd be listening to sirens, horns blaring, and other traffic noise nonstop.

My thoughts kept me awake until long past midnight. When sleep did come, it was filled with disturbing dreams.

12

I decided not to go for a walk. It would take up far too much time. I needed to get to town and buy a lawnmower and weed-eater, which I'd use to trim around the house, trees and bushes. After a quick breakfast I took off in the orchard truck.

I actually preferred driving the truck. It seemed to suit me better than my Buick, which I'd hardly driven since the funeral. I was beginning to notice more and more the little dents and dings in the silver finish of my car and the beginnings of rust along the bottom. It was in need of a new set of tires and had close to ninety thousand miles on the odometer. It was definitely time to think about something new.

Within an hour I was back. After I checked that everything was working properly I headed to the barn to get the tractor. The barn was a two-story building, faded red with a metal roof. The large double doors had been left open on the upper level. Inside, the tractor was parked in the middle with stacks of wooden apple crates on one side, bales of hay on the other.

As I entered the darkened barn I looked at the hay and felt a sharp knot forming in my stomach. I stopped and stared up at the orderly pile of bales, suddenly unable to move.

It was all still there.

The rank smell of sweat. The sting of sunburn. The angry words.

The disappointment.

All the pain I had been trying to avoid was there in the barn.

Quickly I slammed the door on the memory of that fateful day. Forcing myself to get on the tractor and start it up I felt myself shaking. As the engine roared and I left the barn, I told myself I'd let my guard down. I needed to be more careful. Soon I'd be back in Chicago away from all the memories. I just needed to hang on a bit longer.

Still shaking I drove to the open shed where dad kept his larger equipment. Backing up to the hay mower with the tractor so I could attach it was a bit tricky. I hadn't done that in years. I finally got the hang of it and with everything in place I headed towards the house. I stopped for a moment and looked out across the lawn. It seemed a shame to mow down all the wildflowers, but it needed to be done.

Mowing in front and back of the house took me over two hours and the monotony of it calmed me down. First I cut going one direction. Then I went at it again from the opposite way. I found myself wishing dad had owned a brush hog.

Once done, I stopped for lunch. It was hot, so I had a cold beer to go with it. It was tempting to call it a day. The sun was beating down and the temperature was in the eighties; on the porch it was cool and shady. But I didn't want to disappoint Janet. She wanted this looking good by the time we had the auction, so I got up and returned to work.

I raked and raked. After several trips with a wheelbarrow full of cut grass and weeds which I dumped in piles behind the chicken coop, I decided the process was too slow. I hooked a hay wagon to the tractor and brought it out to the yard where I spent the rest of the afternoon piling it high with clumps of grass and dead bushes I'd dug up. I trimmed the rose bush and took out the weeds and grass around it. Then I gave it a large drink of water.

By the time I'd added the last of the debris to the wagon and dumped it on top of the previous piles behind the coop, it was late afternoon. I was done for the day. Soaking wet with sweat I only wanted a shower and another beer. I'd finish the mowing and trimming the next day.

Before I could go into the house, though, a white pickup truck came rolling up the driveway, coming to a stop next to the tractor. On the door in dark blue letters it said 'J & J Builders'. Two men dressed in newer jeans, crisp white shirts, and ball caps got out. With big grins on their faces they tried, but failed, to act casual. Even before they reached me they had their hands out introducing themselves. I had no idea who they were, but I went on alert. I'd seen my share of slick salesmen in the insurance business.

"Nice place you've got here. Real pretty," the taller one said looking around with his hands on his hips. "Looks like you've been working hard. Too hard for a hot day like this," he added, as if I might never have realized that on my own.

I wanted to say, "Let's just cut to the chase." I thought I knew what they were about.

"We heard this place might be for sale," the shorter man said as he handed me a business card.

"Yes, we plan to sell…eventually." I didn't want him to think we were having a fire sale.

"Well, my partner and I are developers," the taller one said removing his dark sunglasses. "We're always looking for nice property to build on, and let me tell you, this is a nice piece of land you've got here. I hope you don't mind, but we looked up the specs on your property and we've driven by it a couple times. We really like what we see."

"And just what did you see?" I asked icily.

"A good place to build family homes on five acre parcels. People could live in the country, but still be close to Muskegon or Grand Rapids. A nice place to raise a family—"

"I don't think we'd be interested," I said cutting him off.

"May I ask who owns this with you?" I'm sure he had already looked that up, too.

"My sister, but I doubt she would be interested either."

"Well, at least give her this," the shorter one said, handing me an envelope with their company logo on it. "It's our offer. Share it with your sister. You might change your mind once you see it. It's hard to sell farmland right now. We could close the deal in thirty days. Cash. The place would be out of your hair and you could get on with your lives." He grinned. You'd have thought he had just handed me a winning lottery ticket.

"I think you'll like our offer," the other one smiled, self-assured. "Check it out. Phone number's on the card. We'll let the two of you talk and get back to you in a couple of days."

"Nice meeting you," the taller man said shaking my hand again. Then they got back in their truck, backed around, and gave me a little wave as they drove off.

I went in the house, grabbed a beer and my phone, and headed for the porch. I opened the envelope and read the offer. It was a lot of money. But then, I really didn't know what the land was worth. I knew Janet would though. As I dialed her number I hoped to God she wouldn't be interested in this deal. Yes, it would be good to sell quickly—but not to land developers!

I filled Janet in on the builders. I was relieved when she quietly said, "I don't want to do that, Patrick."

"I don't either, but I need to at least tell you what the offer is, in all fairness, so you know what I know." Then I read it to her.

"That's not a great offer, Patrick," she said after I'd finished. "I know it has to be worth more than that. I guess we could live with it if we had to, but I think we can do better. I hate to think of it all being developed—in fact, I abhor the idea if I'm being truthful. But we need to be realistic. Let's set the offer aside. It will be our choice of last resort."

"Can I set it aside in a waste basket?" I asked.

"No," she laughed. "But I know how you feel. This is not the way we want to leave the farm behind if we don't have to."

"Let's hope we never get to that point," I said. "See you Friday, Sis."

The work went much quicker the next day after having gotten everything cut shorter the day before. I was done by early afternoon and decided to have a little snack. I sat down at the kitchen table with a book and an apple. Dolly came over, tail wagging, bumping her nose under my arm trying to get to the apple. I tried pushing her away, but she was determined.

"So, you're trying to tell me you want this apple," I said. "Seriously?"

She continued pushing against my arm. Going to the counter I saw dad's jack knife sitting by the canisters, the once shiny finish of the knife worn dull by long time use. I grabbed it and sat back down.

"You'll have to share," I said. "Part of this is mine."

I cut the apple into quarters and began slicing off pieces which Dolly took gingerly between her teeth from my fingers. Suddenly another memory wandered in, as they had for days now; random thoughts that seemed to materialize out of nowhere, often for no apparent reason.

It was early last September. I'd been at Janet's for the Labor Day long weekend. I hadn't planned on stopping to see dad, but when I came to the turnoff to the farm I found myself heading in that direction. I heard his tractor out in the orchard and made my way to the row he was working on. He was setting out empty apple boxes for the picking that would soon take place. He saw me and turned off the engine and got down. We made small talk, as usual. About the weather. About the apple crop. About the migrant workers he had hired.

As we talked I watched my dad reach up through the leafy branches, squinting against the bright afternoon sunlight peeking through the tree. He selected his prize—a crimson orb that just fit in his palm. He wiped the apple thoroughly on his green work pants, the ones he always wore along with a green work shirt and cap—a uniform of sorts—produced a jack knife from his back pocket and deftly cut the apple into quarters. He laid each piece on the fender of his orchard tractor, the old John Deere with the put-put engine. Choosing one quarter he quickly removed the core, cut off a slice, then lifted it to his mouth—knife still in hand. When he finished chewing he cut off the next slice. I watched mesmerized as he continued slicing and chewing until the apple was gone; each time I flinched as the knife blade passed by his eyes. Snack completed, he wiped the knife on his sleeve, closed it and returned it to his pocket. "Time's a wastin'," he said and climbed back on the tractor.

He proceeded down the rutted row of trees, showing me his back as he bounced up and down on the tractor seat. I stood and watched until he disappeared from sight. Once again I wished Nora had been with me. She'd a way with dad that neither Janet nor I ever did. I knew if she'd been with me he wouldn't have dismissed me so abruptly and gone back to work.

I gave the last slice of the apple to Dolly, and then started to return the jack knife to the counter. Then I hesitated. After standing there weighting the knife in my hand, I finally rubbed it on my pants, closed it, and put it in my pocket.

When Janet arrived Friday morning she was pleased at how everything looked.

"My goodness, Patrick, it doesn't look so deserted anymore. This really makes it look like home again. And you're so tan!"

"It was a hot job, but I guess it was worth it."

"Oh, it was," she said giving me a quick hug. She went to her car and returned with a sign placing it near the porch steps: "For Sale by Owner".

"Now what?" I asked.

"We need to get ready for the auction. His guys will carry out the heavy stuff. They'll be here by six tomorrow morning to get set up, so they can carry out the china cabinet and other furniture. But I need you to help me with something. I've decided I want to keep the trunk that mom used to store her wedding dress. Can you help me carry it down and put it in the back of my SUV?"

"Good Lord, Janet, that's got to be heavy." Then seeing the look in her eyes, I added, "But I guess the two of us can manage." We carried the trunk down the attic steps, then struggled with it down the steps to the first floor, and finally out to Janet's car. After that we spent several hours packing boxes and stacking them on the porch to be carried out to the lawn in the morning for the auction.

Before she left that afternoon we sat for a while in lawn chairs in the shade of the maple tree. Looking around Janet said, "There's just got to be a better way than letting this land get developed. I can't get that off my mind. I hope they were wrong about farmland being hard to sell."

"That was probably just a sales tactic to scare us. But I can't get it off my mind either."

"Well, neither of us is destitute, so I say let's not make any quick decisions. We do need to come to an agreement, though, on what we would accept as an offer."

"I'll get on the computer tonight and see if I can come up with some numbers," I offered.

"And I'll go back to Mary Beth's and call my bank. I have a friend there that may be able to help. We can compare notes in the morning."

That evening I spent some time investigating what other farm land had sold for in our area and came to the conclusion that the land developers' offer was definitely much lower than the land was worth. It angered me that they were trying to take advantage of people who had just gone through a loss. And I knew it wasn't the first time.

Chapter 12

I couldn't sleep again that night. The porch was full of boxes, so I sat in dad's recliner going through the old letters. Most of them mom had saved, many of which were from her mother. The Olmstead's had lived in northern Michigan and we seldom saw them, but it looked like Grandma Olmstead had kept in touch regularly. The letters, though, held little interest for me; I read details of neighbors I didn't know, recipes, gardening tips, and the goings on at grandma's church. I'm sure it meant a lot to my mom that she'd heard from her mother so often. The letters did give me some insight into what my grandparents were like, though, and the kind of lives they'd led. I knew Janet would enjoy reading them, so I set them aside to for her.

There were letters from friends of mom's that she knew before she was married. Mom had been a nurse until she married dad, so many of her friends were also nurses. They wrote about work, new boyfriends, marriages, and children. There were invitations to weddings, showers, and notes with baby pictures inside.

Then I came to a letter with a return address from Boston. It had been addressed to my dad. I didn't recognize the name of the sender. Thinking of the last envelope I'd opened, I hoped there wasn't going to be any unwanted surprises. Probably not. Most likely it had something to do with the farm. Maybe he had ordered something. But why keep it? I saw the date stamp on the front of the envelope and became curious. It had been sent in 1945. Well, whatever it was, it was from a long time ago.

Carefully I slipped the contents out of the envelope into my lap. There was a letter folded in half; placed inside the fold a yellowed news clipping and a small black and white photo peeked out. Another photo I thought.

I picked up the photo and studied it. Looking back at me were two men in army uniforms, caps at a rakish angle, smiling for the camera. I'd never seen any army photos of my father, but there was no mistaking that one of those men was my dad. Turning it over revealed the names written on the back. "Paddy and Sam".

Then it dawned on me. Paddy was probably a nickname for Patrick. This was the man I'd been named after.

Looking at the news clipping I realized it was an obituary.

13

The auction was a long event. I thought the day would never end. Nearly a hundred people showed up; most were men, but some of the farmer's wives came as well. The auctioneer moved from place to place as he sold machinery, tools, and even the bales of hay in the barn. Some of dad's machinery was quite old and we got very little for it. As the tractors and hay wagon and plows and all the other pieces of farm equipment were bid on and sold, I felt a pang in my stomach. This is what both Janet and I had agreed on, but it didn't feel right. I kept telling myself when people died things had to be liquidated; but it felt terribly sad that in just a few hours everything that had kept this farm going by my father would be gone.

The auction finished up about three o'clock. Janet and I had done a lot of standing around and were glad for things to wrap up. The few people left milling about were farmers visiting with each other before they got in their vehicles and left. Three of those remaining were Ed, Henry, and Junior. Ed finally came over and asked if they could have a word with Janet and me. Janet was signing paperwork with the auctioneer, but I told him as soon as she was finished we could talk.

We moved on to the porch out of the heat and Janet brought out a pitcher of lemonade. I was tired and anxious for everyone to be gone. I knew Janet felt the same, but when Ed said he wanted to talk to us about the land, he suddenly had our attention.

I wondered if we were about to get an offer, and if we were, would it be one we'd be willing to accept. We certainly liked Ed and his family well enough. They'd been invaluable to us since dad had died. But were they looking for a deal? I wondered if they'd gotten wind of the land developers. I'm sure they wouldn't want a subdivision bordering their property. I was nervous.

"We've done some hard thinkin' the last few days," Ed said. 'Henry and Junior are wantin' to buy the land and split it. You see, Junior here, is gettin' married soon and wants a place of his own."

"Congratulations, Junior," Janet and I said at the same time. She and I quickly made eye contact. We'd been thinking the same thing. How much will they offer and would we be happy with it?

"But my bride-to-be, Judy, don't want the farm house," Junior interrupted. "She wants me to build her a new house. I'm hopin' we can work somethin' out."

Janet told him not to worry about the house. She'd already filed paperwork to split it and five acres off to be sold separately. He seemed relieved. We could tell he really wanted the land, but he also had a fiancée to please."

"If it were up to me," he said, "I could live here just fine. I'm not saying it's not a nice house, but she wants somethin' more to her likin'. She likes more modern things. I'd probably cut down most of the apple orchard, though, and I don't know how you feel about that. Judy has a spot picked out where she wants me to build a house. She wants to keep some of them apple trees around the new place, but I'd really not be needin' more'n a few. I'd be building me a new barn, too."

"We understand," I replied. "Truthfully, Junior, getting rid of the orchard comes as no big surprise to us. We know most people would probably cut it down and plow it up for farm land. It's sad, but we need to be realistic. That's the way farming's going now. Unless you have a large orchard it's hard to make it as an orchard grower anymore."

"And the trees here are getting old and not so productive anymore," Janet added. There were nods of agreement all around.

I asked Henry, "How about your prospects? Have you any girlfriends in the wings?"

"No way. I'm a confirmed bachelor and I 'tend on stayin' that way. I'm perfectly happy livin'with mom and dad."

"He'll get half the farm when the missus and I pass on," Ed said. "That way, both my boys will have a place of their own. Between the two of 'em they'll have plenty of acreage to farm.

Then Ed made his offer.

Janet and I having done our investigations and talking things over that morning, and knowing what the proposal from the developers had been, knew Ed's offer was fair. Janet looked at me and nodded.

"You've got a deal," I said smiling. We shook hands all around. We drank another round of lemonade, then they left saying they had to get back home to do their chores. I looked at Janet and saw tears in her eyes.

"It's been saved, Patrick. All of it. Everything here that we love will not be gouged out for streets and slapped over with concrete. We thought the house and five acres would be sold first, but no one even mentioned the for sale sign on the lawn."

"It sure surprised the heck out of me, too. I'm as relieved as you are," I said, thinking about the woods and the creek and all the other beautiful parts of the farm. Then suddenly I started getting choked up.

"What's wrong, Patrick?"

"I'm sorry. I'm surprised I'm getting so emotional about this. I didn't think I had any big attachment to the farm. But today seeing the machinery going, selling the land, it all seems so…well, final. I can't help but wonder…" But I couldn't finish my thought.

"I think you're having seller's remorse, Patrick. That's not unusual. We're both exhausted and things have gone pretty fast the last few days. We've had to make a lot of decisions in a short time. It's a lot to take in."

"Today when all the equipment was being sold did you ever wonder what dad would say about all this?"

"Patrick, if you're feeling guilty about any of this you need to get that right out of your head. There's been enough judging in this family. This has nothing to do with dad anymore. What he might have wanted can't enter into our decisions. You'd only be keeping everything because you'd want to please him. But the only thing that would've ever pleased dad is if you'd come crawling back and said you'd been wrong…and you weren't.

I know it sounds harsh talking that way about our dad, but remember, Patrick, he was my dad, too, and I haven't forgotten what he was like. These are things we've agreed on and I think we've made the right decisions."

"I do, too. I'm sorry."

"No need to be sorry. But I do know what you mean about everything feeling final. Don't think for a minute I haven't thought about how hard it's going to be going out the driveway one last time knowing that I can never come back to mom and dad's place.

14

The day after the auction I sat at the kitchen table having coffee when I heard Janet's car come up the driveway. It was after ten. She was late, but that didn't matter. I'd slept in myself that morning and had my own difficulty getting up and moving.

Janet came in and sat down across from me hugging a mug of coffee. I looked at the dark circles under her eyes.

"You don't look so good," I said.

"Gee, thanks. I needed that this morning."

"If it's any consolation, I feel the same way.'"

We talked for a while about the auction, the things that sold and the things that didn't, and, of course, we talked about the surprise offer from Henry and Junior. We were still trying to take it all in when I said, "Janet, have you had breakfast yet?"

"No, I barely made it out of bed."

"Well, me either. How about you let your brother buy you breakfast? We haven't really had much time to just sit and talk to each other, and when we do it's always about the farm. I'll take you into town to Sally's Café and buy you breakfast and we can just chill out."

For a moment she said nothing, thinking about the work we should be doing; then she smiled. "That's the best offer I've had in a long time."

"Besides," I said, "there's something I want to show you." As we left I picked up my laptop. "I hope they have Wi-Fi there."

Sally's Café was usually packed on Sunday mornings, but the crowd had been there and gone by the time we arrived. Janet and I found a booth by a window and prepared to just take our time. I ordered eggs, sausage, and hash browns, along with homemade biscuits. Janet had a vegetarian omelet. I was happy to have someone to eat with for a change and to eat someone else's cooking.

After the waitress cleared away our dishes and refilled our coffee I got out the envelope I wanted to share. I pulled out the photo, but before I could hand it to her Janet had her hand up to stop me, almost spilling her coffee.

"Oh, no….not another picture. I don't know if I want to see it. Please don't tell me we have an older sister, too," she said.

I laughed, "No, but I had the same reaction when I first came across it, worried about what it might be. But I think you'll find this more interesting than upsetting."

I handed it to her and watched while she studied it, then turned it over to the back.

"Is this who I think it is?" she asked.

"Well, if you think it's the guy I was named after, then I'm pretty sure you're right."

"Look how young they are. They're just kids."

"Basically, most of them were when you think about it."

"Dad looks so handsome. Well, Patrick does, too."

"There were some other things in the envelope with the photo. If you read this it will tell you something about the guy." I handed her the obituary. She took her time reading it.

The Boston Herald, February 15, 1945

Sgt. Patrick Donavan Murphy, son of Mr. and Mrs. Patrick Murphy Sr. of Boston, was killed in action December 27, 1944 in the Ardennes Forest, Luxembourg, when the Allied Forces faced a surprise attack from German forces. Since receiving the news about their son, the Allied forces have since retaken the area. Sgt. Murphy was born August 8, 1923 and enlisted in the army in 1941. Before leaving for the service Mr. Murphy worked at the Boston Navy Yard as a dock worker and was a member of the St. Stephens Church. He held the rank of Technical Sergeant in the 328th Infantry 26th Division under the leadership of General George Patton. He leaves behind a sister, Kathleen, 14, and two sets of grandparents, Mr. and Mrs. Thomas Murphy and Mr. and Mrs. William Ryan, all from Boston. Burial took place at the American Cemetery in Luxembourg. Sgt. Murphy was posthumously awarded the Silver and Bronze medals and the Purple Heart.

Janet laid the clipping on the table and quietly said, "That's certainly someone to be named after, Patrick."

"I'd say it would be someone hard to live up to…but of course, I never knew he existed. Maybe in dad's mind I was supposed to be like him."

"Patrick, you don't know that."

"I know, but the thought runs through my mind."

Wanting to change the subject she asked, "Why did you bring the laptop?"

"I want to show you something, but first read the letter that was in the envelope with the photo. It was written by Patrick's mother." Janet unfolded the letter and read:

Dear Samuel,

My husband and I want you to know how much your letter has meant to us. It was with some relief that you told us Patrick did not suffer. Though it cannot take away our awful pain, it does ease it some. Patrick wrote of you often and considered you a special friend in a time of war. It is comforting to know you were with him in the last moments of his life here on earth. I am enclosing a copy of his obituary and a photo of the two of you that was in his belongings when they were returned to us. God bless you for all you have done in very difficult times.

Sincerely,
Mrs. Patrick Murphy, Sr.

"Dad was there when Patrick died," she said barely able speak as she thought about what he had been through. She handed the letter back to me. "I can't even imagine what that had to have felt like. And to think he took the time to write his friend's parents a letter. It doesn't sound much like our dad, does it? But then, we've never been told anything about dad being in the war. He never talked about it. Neither did mom. They say war changes people. It makes me wonder what he was like before that. Mom didn't know him before the war did she?"

"No, I'm pretty sure they met after he came back home."

"Do you know anything about this battle, Patrick?" she asked.

"That's why I brought my laptop along. I've done some research. They were in "The Battle of the Bulge," I said, turning on the computer.

"I've heard of that. It was really bad."

"It was the largest and bloodiest battle of World War II."

"And dad was there," she said softly to herself, pushing aside her cold coffee.

"Okay, I'll read you some of the details. It says it started December 16, 1944 and lasted until January 30, 1945. The Allies were surprised by an attack from the Germans... let's see... due to bad weather the Allied planes were grounded so there had been no aerial reconnaissance...the Ardennes Forest was very dense and the few roads there were impassable...the American troops had to wade through deep snow to counterattack. I've read some accounts of soldiers that said the cold was unbearable."

"That's a long time from the middle of December to the end of January," Janet commented.

"No kidding. The Germans were trying to push through the Allied lines and because at first they were succeeding there was a bulge in the lines, thus the name, 'Battle of the Bulge'."

"But they stopped them?"

"Yes, but it was costly. Says here that the Department of Defense estimated there were nearly 90,000 American casualties, with 19,000 killed, 47,000 wounded and 23,000 captured or missing."

"My God! To think dad could have been one of them; and the things he must have seen..."

"The Germans didn't fare well, either. Estimates were....let me see...okay, 80,000 to 100,000 casualties, 30,000 captured or killed. They lost a lot of military equipment, especially aircraft. It was the beginning of the end for them."

"All those people killed on both sides---it's no wonder dad never wanted to talk about it."

I turned the computer so she could see a picture of the American Cemetery in Luxembourg.

"So Patrick is buried there?" she said.

"Yes, but he was far from alone. Take a look." I brought up another photo of the cemetery showing the rows and rows of white crosses.

I knew dad had been in the war, that's why the local VFW had been at his funeral, but I had no details and really never thought much about it since he never talked about it. My one attempt to learn anything had been squashed when I asked mom about my name. I wished I had known more.

We stayed for a while longer, nursing coffees, talking about what we'd learned, family, and things we remembered growing up. It felt good to talk with no agenda. When it was time to head back to the farm, I suggested we take a walk to the creek before Janet left to go back home.

"Lots of wildflowers are blooming," I said. I thought Janet might decide she was too tired, but she perked up at the idea.

"I haven't been there in years," she said.

15

We started down the lane with Dolly happily trotting alongside us. The lane was one vehicle wide. It had become rough and rutted where tires had worn it down, leaving the center between the tracks covered with grass and weeds. Janet was wearing her sandals which made walking difficult, but she waved off the idea of waiting to go another other day. It was a beautiful Sunday afternoon with a slight breeze. The perfect time for a walk.

It took longer for us to get to the woods than usual. Janet had to stop and examine every flower and bush along the way.

In the lane she paused near a patch of Queen Anne's lace just beginning to blossom. Several swallowtail butterflies were darting around them. The wide flat flowers really did remind me of lace. They were one of the few wildflowers I recognized by name, mostly because they were a favorite of my mother. She sometimes called them 'wild carrots'.

"Do you remember what mom used to do with Queen Anne's lace?" Janet asked.

"I know she used to press them between pieces of wax paper and put them in books to dry."

"Yes, but I'm thinking about something else. She would cut them and put them in Mason jars with water and food coloring. The next day she'd have red, purple, and blue Queen Anne's lace."

"I'd forgotten about that," I said with a smile. "But now I remember her setting them on the windowsill over the kitchen sink."

Janet stopped at a cluster of cedar. She pointed out the damage done by deer over the winter.

"Cedar is like candy to deer," she said.

She commented on the dense areas of sassafras trees as we pushed past the locust and choke cherry bushes, bees singing in our ears.

"It sure has grown up a lot around here since we lived at home, hasn't it?" I said as we continued our slow pace.

When we finally stepped into the woods we disturbed a number of squirrels who hastily made it to the closest trees. Dolly wasn't sure which one she should chase. We were warm from the walk and the cool of the woods was a gentle relief. You could smell the dampness in the air.

Janet spied an area of Mayapples. "It's a little early," she said, "otherwise this would be the perfect spot to start hunting morel mushrooms." At the mention of mushrooms my mouth watered; there was nothing like morels sautéed in butter.

We walked further into the woods. Our feet were made crunching and rustling sounds on the twigs and dead leaves from last fall. We wouldn't be sneaking up on any animals or birds. Well, having Dolly with us didn't help either, but it didn't seem right to go for a walk without her. Walking with Janet was like having my own personal tour guide. When Janet was growing up she had made it a point to learn the names of every living thing around us. Her memory hadn't failed her. She was happy to be in the woods again, falling back on old times.

After a while she said, "Wow, I haven't seen these in a long time." I made no comment. Obviously I wasn't impressed enough so she added, "They're called Jack in the pulpit."

We continued on to the log I usually sat on, but Janet wanted to keep looking. I sat down watching her. Many times she squatted down and cupped a small flower in her hands. Then she said, "Come look at this."

"What is it?" I asked trying to show the right amount of enthusiasm, I leaned over a small white flower.

"It's called trillium. It's a protected flower. In fact, there are lots of plants here that are protected. Don't pick them, Patrick."

I assured her I had no intention of picking anything.

I returned to the log while she made it down the slippery bank and disappeared from sight for several minutes. When she came back up to sit beside me, she was out of breath. She began naming off other plants she had seen: lady slippers, marsh marigolds and a large mound of forget-me-nots. There's blue iris growing right into the water's edge," she said adding, "This walk was such a good idea."

Clearly Janet was in sensory overload.

We sat in silence enjoying each other's company and the sounds of the woods and creek. In the distance we heard the loud cry of a pileated woodpecker, and then saw its large awkward body swoop over the trees. Chickadees and goldfinches darted about the trees, going from limb to limb. The peacefulness was finally broken by Dolly who had spied a black squirrel sitting on a low branch in a nearby poplar tree. Dolly sat looking up at the squirrel. It sat staring down at Dolly and screeched its annoyance.

I told Janet about the heron I'd seen.

"Did you know herons mate for life?" she asked.

"Hmm…no, I didn't know that. But I'm thinking heron relationships are probably a lot less complicated than human ones."

She laughed. "I think you're right." Then she added, "I used to see kingfishers here."

"I remember seeing those, but I haven't seen any since I've been back."

"They were so amazing the way they'd dive head first into the water, making that rat-a-tat-tat sound like a machine gun. They used to make me laugh."

"Maybe they're all gone," I said.

She sighed. "I hope not. Our world's changing…"

I expected a lecture on climate change, deforestation, or pollution, but instead she said, "Let's walk a little more."

She began naming off a number of trees. I wondered if Janet was testing herself to make sure she hadn't forgotten anything. Box elder, swamp oak, cotton wood, and red maple. She stopped and felt their bark in a caressing way as if they were old friends.

"I hate living in Lansing," she said as we started the walk back. "I never realized how much until now. Don't get me wrong. Lansing is a nice place to live. But I liked it so much better when we lived in our old house. I had some beautiful gardens there. But Phil had to move to a larger, more expensive house in an exclusive neighborhood. He pays to have someone else take care of the yard and gardens. He gets mad if I try to add plants of my own. I'm just not the manicured-lawn type; I'd be a lot happier living in the middle of the woods," she laughed. "Like that's ever going to happen."

Chapter 15

Once we returned to the house, Janet hugged me. "This has been the best day I've had in a long time," she said before getting into her car and heading off.

After she left, I spent the rest of Sunday afternoon on the porch reading a book with Dolly by my side. Janet had looked so much more relaxed when she left. I felt as if I'd given her a gift, yet I'd done nothing more than suggest we go for breakfast and a walk.

16

After days of dragging a ladder around the house cleaning leaf litter out of the eave troughs, and scraping and painting windowsills, I had been preparing to mow the lawn once again. It was an overcast day. Heavy low-hanging clouds began piling up in the west. They had grown darker by the moment and the wind had quickly picked up, so Dolly and I took refuge on the porch. She was gnawing on her chewy and I was drinking lukewarm coffee as usual.

I had been making notes in my notebook, but then I turned to the section on mom. I took out her photo from the pocket folder, the one with her holding the enormous watermelon. Janet was right. Mom did have a beautiful smile. I tucked it back in the pocket and started to write when my pen ran out of ink.

Reaching inside my bag for a new one I saw the American poetry book and pulled it out. I noticed the corner of one page was dog-eared. I wondered what mom had been reading and thought special enough to mark. She must have read it often as the book fell open naturally to that page. What it revealed was a pleasant surprise; a Queen Anne's lace had been pressed between layers of waxed paper and inserted between the pages. It was yellowed, but still in remarkably good shape. I studied it for a moment imagining my mom picking the flower and deciding to keep it. Of all the Queen Anne's lace, why had she chosen this one? I carefully removed the fragile flower and placed it inside one of my grandfather's books for safe keeping.

Returning to the page of poetry I saw tea stains and smudges. I was sure this poem had held some special significance for her. It was a poem by Robert Frost, "The Road Not Taken". I read it aloud thinking of my mom sitting in her chair at night reading this and wondered what she thought as she came to the last stanza:

> *I shall be telling this with a sigh*
> *Somewhere ages and ages hence;*
> *Two roads diverged in a wood, and I—*
> *I took the one less traveled by,*
> *And that has made all the difference.*

I wondered what had been the significance of this poem. Had mom chosen a road for which she had regrets? My mom had taken a conventional path when she had given up nursing to marry my dad. Was she was sorry about that choice, or was there something else she had wanted but never achieved. I wished I could ask her. She was so insistent that Janet use her scholarship and go to college. Live her dream. For Janet to be careful which road she chose. I could understand how disappointed mom had been when Janet had quit college after her first year.

I hoped mom hadn't had a lot of regrets. I knew Janet had. And regret and I were well acquainted. Sitting there with the poetry book open in my lap, I started thinking back to one choice in particular. I'd never considered at the time how it was going to affect me. It had set off a series of choices that had followed me the rest of my life.

The year after mom died was an extremely difficult time for me. Maybe if I'd been a little older I would've handled things better, but as it was, my mood would often sink to such lows that I barely hung on. Mom had always been my life-line, encouraging me to do new things, making me feel as if I had some importance. Living alone with dad was suffocating.

I felt like little more than a hired hand. I came home from school and helped with the chores. I cooked meals which we ate in silence. I cleaned up the kitchen by myself while dad retired to his chair with the newspaper. Then I sat at the kitchen table and did my homework. By nine o'clock dad was on his way to bed. The routine rarely varied.

Once my homework was out of the way and dad was asleep, I started meeting up with Buddy and Charlie. Dad had to know I left the house every night, but he never told me I couldn't. We'd hang out, drink and smoke some, and look for girls. Charlie had a car by then, so we were free to roam. I was always home by midnight and up by five thirty in the morning, no matter how tired or hung-over I was, to help with the morning chores and get off to school on time.

One evening in May, close to graduation, we'd been driving around, bored and looking for something to do. It was pretty quiet in Brooks Creek.

"I sure wish we could find a party, but we'd have to bring our own beer. I don't know about you, but I'm broke," Buddy said.

"I know where we can get some beer—or maybe something harder," Charlie suggested.

"What? Where'd we get something like that with no money? You gotta a stash hidden someplace?" Buddy asked.

"No…but I know a window that's not locked."

"What are you talking about?" I wanted to know.

"Well, I was in Grayson's Party Store this afternoon buying a coke and some chips. I asked if I could use the bathroom. It's way in the back of the store, you know. And it has a window."

"You're not talking about breaking in, are you? That's crazy!" I was shocked. "We can't do that!"

"Actually, it's not breaking in," he said. "I unlocked the window before I left. I checked before I met up with you guys tonight. The store's closed, but the window's still unlocked."

"So…you propose we do what?" Buddy asked.

I couldn't believe Buddy wanted any part of this.

"We just go in, maybe each of us take a six pack, then leave. Mr. Grayson will never notice a little beer gone missing."

I didn't like the idea at all, but Buddy said, "Are you sure we can fit through the window? As I remember it's pretty small."

"Well, that's why we need Patrick here. I'm, too big. Don't think you'll fit either, Bud; but Mr. Slim here," he said, patting me on the shoulder, "I think he'll fit."

Everything screamed at me to say no, but after a little more convincing we were headed towards town and the party store in Charlie's Camaro. It was bright red with duel exhaust. Not exactly the best choice for a get-away car.

We parked a couple blocks away and walked through the alley to the back of the store. Once I squeezed inside I handed three six packs out the window to Charlie and Bud.

"Get a carton of cigarettes while you're at it," Charlie said. I hesitated. This was getting worse by the moment. "Come on, get a move-on."

I handed him the cigarettes and started climbing out the window, but Charlie stopped me. Looking around he said, "One more thing, Patrick. Grab a couple bottles of the hard stuff."

"What! I've got to get out of here! I've done enough!"

"Shhh…Just do it and we can go."

I pulled myself back through the window and into the store. I didn't know what to get so I grabbed a bottle of some kind of whisky and a bottle of rum.

We quickly headed back to the car and made our way to the beach where several other kids, mostly seniors, were already celebrating. The beach at Lake Michigan had always been a hangout, especially on warm summer nights. There among the dunes and beach grass we'd drag up drift wood to sit on, build bonfires, laugh, talk and listen to music into the early morning. Some guys we knew had a bonfire going so we joined them. Charlie asked if anyone had some glasses, and soon we were drinking and making dumb toasts to our graduation and freedom. It was a good time…until the sheriff showed up.

It seemed a lady living in the house behind Grayson's saw me climbing out of the window. She threw on her bathrobe and followed us to Charlie's car. It took a while for Mr. Grayson to get to the store. He did have a pretty good idea of what was missing, despite what Charlie had said about us not needing to worry.

The police had gone to the beach looking for Charlie's car and a party. They were well acquainted with his car, having stopped him several times for excessive speed.

Once there, it didn't take long for Buddy to spill his guts. It was a long drive to the police station in the back of the patrol car. Buddy and Charlie's parents were called, but they weren't able to reach my dad. He probably couldn't hear the phone from the upstairs bedroom. Buddy and Charlie were picked up by their parents and taken home, and then a patrol car drove me out to the farm. It was past midnight when the officer left me in the patrol car and pounded on the door, waking up my dad.

Once the officer had explained why he was there and left, I stood waiting for all hell to break loose. But nothing happened. Dad just stood there and stared at me without saying a word. Then he turned around and walked back upstairs to bed. That was worse than if he had yelled at me. His look had said it all.

In the weeks that followed dad and I talked even less, if that was possible. Mr. Grayson didn't press charges. He said he would consider it a high school graduation prank if we agreed to work off the money for what was stolen. Each of us was given jobs to do on the weekends. I mostly worked on Sundays, raking leaves in Mrs. Grayson's yard or helping put in her vegetable garden. And after that, I still had my usual chores at home.

While I was working I had time to think about what I wanted to do after graduation. I had decent grades, so I started making plans for college. I still wanted to become a journalist.

I couldn't wait to get away from home and start my own life.

17

I continued to visit the creek every morning. It had become my writing sanctuary. There, away from worries about the work to be done, I was able to write. I filled the first notebook and was well into the second one. I recounted the stealing incident at Grayson's in much detail; then I wrote about graduation which was two weeks later. Standing in line in the auditorium wearing my cap and gown along with my classmates, I glanced around looking for my dad. When I caught Janet's eyes, she just shook her head. I already knew there would be no after-graduation party, but that he would not show up for the ceremony was something I hadn't even considered. Sensing my disappointment, Charlie's dad, Mr. Carpenter, invited me back to their home and Charlie's party. I stayed for about an hour, but my heart wasn't in it. I went home and began my chores early.

When I returned to the house with Dolly that morning I saw another basket of eggs Ed had left on the doorstep. Those leg-horns really must be productive. Seeing the basket of eggs reminded me of my mother. When she was alive we raised a lot of chickens. We sold the eggs to neighbors, people who drove out from town, and to Clauson's grocery store. My mom had spent hours at the sink washing baskets of eggs, weighing them, and placing them in cardboard egg cartons. Once she was gone, we only kept enough chickens for our own use.

But I was sick of eating eggs. I looked in the cabinets and refrigerator and finally came up with enough ingredients to make pancakes. About halfway through the stack I'd had enough. I could eat no more. I took the rest out and scraped them into Dolly's dish.

I busied myself cleaning up the kitchen. I'd just finished washing dishes when I looked out the window and saw Dolly trot past, disappearing behind the shed. Something was hanging from her mouth. Curious, I decided to check out what she was up to.

At the shed I could see her tail sticking out by the back of the barn. Quietly I approached and peeked around the corner. Dolly's front paws were digging furiously and from her jaws hung the offending pancakes. When she saw me she stopped. She looked up with eyes that said she knew she was in trouble. She lowered her head and her tail drooped; she let the pancakes fall to the ground and stood there panting. I couldn't help but laugh at Dolly, worried she was going to be scolded for burying pancakes. Once again I thought about how much I was going to miss this wonderful dog.

"Geez, Dolly," I said, ruffling her fur, "you could have just told me you didn't like pancakes. But you're right. They really weren't all that good." I left her to her job, and headed back to the house to start mine.

As the week passed I worked on my manuscript, usually in the early evening. Stan had been happy with chapter three, thankfully, but I still had other corrections to make, sometimes spending an hour rewriting just one paragraph.

I finished several small jobs on the house. Even though they were not big projects, they were still time consuming. Fixing the broken window in the living room that was held together with packing tape was challenging, but I had gotten advice from the owner of the hardware store on how to do it. His directions were good and as I finished caulking, I felt good about the job I'd done.

Nights were another matter. Nights were filled with worry about the future. About Dolly. About my book—was it really any good? Would I ever write another one? Was Jack going to give me a hard time when I returned to work?

In the living room I often sat with the three photos I'd kept— baby Sam, my mom, and Patrick, and wondered if anything I'd ever done was good enough. I struggled with their ghosts every night. And then there was dad.

I often thought about what my life might have been like if my mom had lived. There was no way to know, but I wanted to believe she would have encouraged me in the same way she had Janet, to go on to college and become a journalist if that's what I wanted. I questioned whether she would have approved of the choices I'd made.

Picking up the photo of baby Sam, it wasn't hard to convince myself I was supposed to have been his replacement. Another son, another chance to fulfill my dad's plans. If Sam had lived would he have wanted to stay on the farm? He might have worked alongside dad the same way Henry and Junior worked with Ed. It's possible he could have grown up, married, and taken over the farm. That sure would've taken pressure off me.

And this guy, I thought, as I picked up Patrick's photo with dad. How do you live up to a war hero? I was doomed before I even started.

It seemed all I did was disappoint people.

Friday Janet was going to be late so I spent the morning cleaning out the basement and attic by carrying everything that was left out to the dumpster. Then I took garbage bags up to my old bedroom, opened the closet door and tossed all the old clothes and shoes into a bag. On the closet shelf I saw two old school yearbooks I hadn't noticed before. I reached up and got them down, placing them on the desk to look at later. I emptied the drawers of clothes, gathered up odds and ends, and left only the items on the desk.

Saturday morning, and I knew time was running out. My job loomed in the distance like a bad dream I was trying hard not to remember.

When Janet arrived she asked, "What are your plans for today?"

"I thought I'd scrub the kitchen cupboards in hopes we could get by without painting them."

She surprised me by agreeing. I think she was as anxious as I was to be finished with everything. She said, "I'm going to go through mom's clothes and finish off that room."

"Well, then, that's what I'm doing, too. I think that's a job we should do together, Sis."

She looked at me and realized I was serious. She nodded. "It would be nice to not do that alone. But I plan on keeping some of those clothes, just so you know."

"Why would you do that? They wouldn't fit you and you said they were so old---"

"Hold on, Patrick. I have a plan. I'll explain it in a minute."

So upstairs we went with more garbage bags. Janet opened the closet door. There were a few clothes left belonging to dad, but he'd mostly worn work clothes, which we'd already tossed out. Janet pulled a summer dress from a hanger, one mom had sewn herself. She tugged on the material and smiled. "This one will work. It's cotton and has held up better than some of the other clothes."

"Okay, are you going to tell me what you're doing?"

"I'm going to make a quilt."

"A quilt?"

"Yes. It's called a memory quilt. When someone you love passes away, you cut up some of their clothing and make a quilt out of it to remember them by."

"I've never heard of that, but it's kind of a nice idea."

"I'm looking mostly for cotton. The colors and prints don't really matter that much. I'll piece them together in a way that I hope will look good."

"Did you see that big quilt book mom had on her book shelf?" I asked.

"Yes, I took it home last night and while thumbing through it I got the idea for the memory quilt. I'm going to sort these clothes out into 'keepers' and 'throw-a ways'," she said putting the sun dress on the bed. While she sorted I cleaned out dad's dresser. When I finished I sat on the bed watching her.

"I'm not sure when I'll make the quilt, but I'm going to be having some extra time on my hands soon," Janet said, adding a flowered skirt to the pile.

"Why is that?"

Janet began telling me about Kelly, her oldest daughter. "She's moving out next weekend."

"Really? Where to?" I asked. Kelly was twenty years old, and of her two daughters, she was the most like Janet.

"She's moving in with her boyfriend, Jason," she said as she folded the clothes she planned on saving. "We like him well enough, and they've dated since high school, but still...I just wanted her to go to college. She says she has no interest in college and is perfectly happy doing what she's doing."

"Is she still working at the bakery?"

"Yes, she said she likes decorating all those wedding and baby shower cakes. It makes her happy to see people excited over what she makes for them."

"Well, that's not all bad, Janet. It means doing something that you like, doesn't it?"

"Yes, but how's she going to make a living decorating cakes?"

"Give her some time, Sis. Maybe she'll tire of it and move on to something better."

"I hope so. And then there's Annie."

"What? Annie's moving, too?

"In a way. She's headed off to college in the fall."

"So, you're going to be an empty nester," I said.

"Yes, just me and Phil in that big house." We let that thought sink in for a moment. "Let's finish up," she said and we moved on.

Mom's shoes were added to a garbage bag along with a couple of purses, their straps cracked from age. Looking up we saw boxes on the top shelf. I took them down and put them on the bed. Janet lifted the lid off one of them.

There wrapped in white tissue paper was mom's nursing cap, still just as white and crisp as the last day she'd worn it.

"That's amazing," I managed to say almost in a whisper. "I've never seen it before."

"Me either," Janet said as she gently lifted it out of the box.

"It must have been really special for her to have kept it," I said. "What should we do with it?"

"I think I'll put it in the trunk with her wedding dress. Let's see what we have in the other box."

Also wrapped in tissue paper was a little blue and white baby sweater with matching cap, booties, and a baby blanket. Janet lifted out a note that lay on top. On paper decorated around the edges with little roses mom had written, 'Our beloved baby Sam'. Next to it was a photo of mom and dad standing in front of the house holding Sam wrapped up in the same baby blanket. He looked like a newborn.

Tears started down Janet's cheeks. I wasn't far behind.

"This is all getting to be too much, don't you think? I mean this whole business of sorting out mom and dad's things, finding all these photos...I'm not sure how much more of this I can take," I said.

"It is hard, but we're close, Patrick. So very close. We've gotten every room cleaned out now. Once we finish the repairs and cleaning I'll call a realtor."

I reached over and hugged her as she said, "This can go in the trunk, too. All these things will be there to tell the story of our mom —nurse, wife, and mother.

We returned to the kitchen where I began making grilled cheese sandwiches for lunch. While I buttered the bread I asked Janet if she had ever heard mom talk about her job as a nurse.

"She loved being a nurse," she said. "She spent most of her time working in the maternity ward. Whenever we were out and she saw a baby, her face would light up. We always had to stop so she could admire the baby and talk to the mother." The talk of babies made me think of Nora, another sad time in my life, but I kept my thoughts to myself.

"Do you think she ever regretted not working as a nurse anymore?" I asked.

Janet thought for a while. "Well, I do remember one argument I overheard between her and dad. It was after you had started school. She wanted to see if she could find work at the hospital."

"And what happened?" I asked.

"About as you would imagine."

"Dad said no."

"Pretty much. He said they didn't need the money, he was supporting the family just fine, and she had plenty of work to do at home."

"He shut her down."

"Yes."

I shook my head. Mom's disappointment hung in the air.

As we ate I looked around the house. It was beginning to feel like a cave. The cupboards and refrigerator were cleaned out of all but necessary items. The other rooms were empty, save a few pieces of worn-out furniture. The walls were bare. Where pictures used to hang there were now blocks of lighter wallpaper outlining where they had hung. It made the ugly wallpaper stand out even more.

"Isn't that the ugliest wallpaper you ever saw?" I asked Janet.

"It was probably pretty and fashionable in its day," she answered.

"I wonder what's under it?"

Janet raised her eyebrows in a way that let me know not to pursue that thought. We already had enough left to do.

Chapter 17

It felt like we had spent weeks erasing everything that had created memories of our parents and our childhood. In some ways, it felt more like a motel, especially at night when I headed off to bed. There were few attachments there anymore. I asked Janet if she felt the same way.

"Yes, it does feel strange. Lonely. Now that we've gotten this far, I can't wait to be done. There's not much here that feels like home anymore.

Janet and I made what we hoped was a final list of what still needed to be done, and continued working our way through some of the jobs the next day.

For days after Janet had gone back to Lansing, I couldn't get the conversation about mom out of my mind. Being alone much of the week the depression had deepened and settled over me like a heavy, wet blanket. I was counting the days until I could return to my old life, such as it was. It had to be less stressful than being forced to confront the past every day.

Then one evening after I'd spent a couple hours puttering around, doing a little bit of this, and a little bit of that, I realized I was just trying to pass the time until I could go to bed to begin another restless night without much sleep. I remembered when Janet had been cleaning out the kitchen cupboards she'd come across a bottle of whisky. She had placed it with the other things that needed to be taken out to the dumpster, which I'd done that night—except I'd kept the whisky and put it back in one of the cupboards. Maybe that would help me sleep. Getting a glass, I went to retrieve it.

Once settled in the dad's recliner, my depression was complete.

I didn't care if I stayed there all night. Pouring myself a drink, I gave in and let go of my defenses, letting the memories of my confrontation with my dad flood over me without restraint.

18

It was mid-July. Dad and I had been hauling hay all day in the scorching sun. The temperature was ninety; the humidity seventy percent. You just couldn't drink enough water. I had been following along behind the hay wagon as dad drove between rows of bales. When he stopped, I would go to one side, hoist bales up onto the wagon, then cross over to the other side and do the same. Now and then I climbed up on the wagon so I could stack the bales higher. I wished I could take my shirt off, but without a shirt I'd get sunburned even worse than I already was, and the sharp cut stalks of hay would jab and scratch my skin making it blotchy and sore. The chaff made me itch something fierce. I prayed for a breeze.

The thick gloves were hot, but kept the twine surrounding the heavy bales from cutting into my hands as I grabbed each one from its resting place in the field. They also protected me from thistles mixed in with the hay, or the occasional snake caught up when the field was baled. If there were a lot of bales in one area dad would hop off the tractor and help me load, but most of the time I was on my own. I was still as lanky as ever, never gaining a pound. But I was strong.

We often worked until the sun went down, sometimes with the tractor lights on, as we were that evening. There was a chance of thunderstorms later that night and the hay couldn't be left out in the rain. As we pulled up to the barn with our last load, I felt relief and the desire for nothing more than a shower, food, and bed—in that order.

Dad came around the front of the tractor. "I noticed there's several fence posts need replacing on the north side," he said, "We'll have to get at them this fall."

It was becoming more apparent each day that dad assumed now that I had graduated I was going to stick around the farm and be his hired-hand. I had been worried about that all summer. Logically, college was the next step for me, but I'd never discussed it with him. I kept putting it off. I knew now I couldn't do that any longer.

"I'll help as much as I can, but part of the time I'll be away at college," I said, trying to brace myself for his response.

"College?" he said, looking over his shoulder at me, a puzzled look on his face.

"Yeah, I plan to go to college this fall. I have a small scholarship and a little money saved, but not near enough. I was hoping you could help me out a little—like you and mom did with Janet."

His back to me, he resumed yanking bales off the wagon. Without turning around he said, "We did that and she quit. Waste of money. You don't need no college education to run a farm."

"I won't quit, I promise," I said to his back, the sharp edge of anger rising in me. I needed to keep it in check. I didn't want this to go wrong, but deep down I knew it was already too late. He wasn't going to dismiss me, though; brush me off like I was no more than a nuisance fly buzzing around his head.

Chapter 18

"After I graduate college I'll start paying you back every cent you loan me…with interest if you want." I hated the desperation in my voice.

He acted as if he hadn't heard me as he unloaded another bale. A question had been burning inside me for weeks now. I wasn't going to like the answer, but I had to know. I couldn't stop myself.

"Why didn't you come to my graduation?"

He turned towards me then, and I could see anger as hot as mine. He resented the question.

"And have all those people stare at me and talk behind my back, whispering about my son the thief?" he spat out. That stung. Tears formed in my eyes mixing with stinging sweat, but I was determined to not let him see me cry.

"That's over and done with. I've learned my lesson. I paid back every cent," my voice rising as I stood my ground. Dad went back to work at the wagon and continued to ignore me. My arms at my sides were shaking as I clenched my fists; my heart hammering in my chest. I was sure I was going to be sick. For a couple minutes I said nothing while I tried without much success to rein in my anger.

Finally taking a breath I said in the calmest voice I could muster, "Look, Dad, I really want to go to college. I've been working towards this all through school."

"Well, you're needed here," he said, as if that was the final word.

Then bridled rage and resentment I'd felt for so long burst out of me in a torrent that surprised even me.

"You don't care about anyone but yourself, do you, Dad? It's not just about the theft. My whole life you've never cared about anything I did, good or bad. Never even a kind word. It's always been about you. What you want. You need to understand what I want for a change. I don't want to be farmer. I never have. I want to be a journalist."

Stepping towards me, he said, "A what?"

"A journalist," I replied, not backing down.

"What kind of job is that?" he sneered as he stared at me with disgust written all over his face. Sweat was running down from under his cap making streaks across his unshaven face. I could smell the odor of unwashed skin and stale breath.

"One I think I'd be good at. I'm really good at writing; everyone says so—"

"Well, if that's what everyone thinks, and you're so fed up with the farm, which by the way has fed and clothed you all these years, well, by all means, go ahead and be one. But you're not doing it on my money—and you're not staying here with all your high-minded ideas either, thinking you're too good to do farm work. I don't need you. You're only worth half a person as it is, hung over as you are most the time. I wouldn't want you to waste your time getting your hands dirty if you can be journalist instead."

With that he kicked a bale out of the way, stormed off to his truck, and drove off.

I stood, unable to move. I watched as dust clouds arched from behind the truck as it headed down the lane. I wasn't sure what to do, but it was out of the question for me to stay there any longer. It would turn into a life sentence. I'd become nothing more than a bitter old man like he was. I'd run out of options. I was so weary of my life.

I went into the house to the upstairs closet, dragged out an old suitcase, and took it to my room where I started throwing in clothes. A few minutes later I was down the stairs and out the door.

Chapter 18

With suitcase in hand, I started the three mile walk to Charlie's house.

19

"You're drunk, Patrick," I said aloud, as I poured myself more whisky. "Mighty, damn drunk."

I thought back to how scared I'd been that night. My whole life had changed in an instant. As I swirled the liquid around in my glass, I stared at the wall across from me at wallpaper that looked as old and worn out as I felt. I noticed a pucker at the top of a seam where the wallpaper had come loose. Just like my life, I thought, after my confrontation with my father. I was at loose ends. I wasn't connected to anything anymore.

Charlie's parents listened as I told them about the argument with my dad. Thankfully, Charlie was out somewhere so he didn't have to witness me trying not to cry in front of his parents. I was so tired, dirty, exhausted, and at the end of my ability to cope I wanted nothing more than to curl up somewhere and close my eyes.

Mr. Carpenter asked, "Did he really tell you to get out?"

"Yes, sir, he told me if I didn't want to farm, I could just leave."

"Charles," Mrs. Carpenter interrupted. "He needs to go back to his father. He can't stay here."

"Just a minute, Lila," he said. "I'm just trying to make sure I understand everything." He asked me several more questions about what led up to the fight. I told him everything, beginning with me asking dad about graduation. Real concern showed on his face.

"I'm going to give his dad a call to let him know where Patrick is; then we'll decide what's best to do. Lila, get this boy something to eat."

So while I ate a grilled cheese sandwich with a glass of milk, trying hard to keep my eyes open, Mr. Carpenter called my dad. When he returned he looked disappointed.

"I'm sorry, Patrick, your dad's a good man, but he's stubborn and a bit prideful. He'll come around in time."

I doubted that, but said nothing.

"In the meantime, you can stay here for a couple days. I think you both need some cooling off time. Then maybe we can talk to him again."

"Charles..."

"Lila, his dad confirmed everything Patrick told us. I think we need to give the boy some help here."

So that's how I came to stay with the Carpenters. Charlie was ecstatic when he found I'd be staying with them. He couldn't get over how much fun it was going to be; all our evenings together out with our friends. But all I wanted was to get some sleep. Secretly I hoped my dad never relented and wanted me back.

I learned later from Charlie that after a week went by with no word from my dad, Mr. Carpenter had gone over to the farm to talk with him. Afterwards he had made a decision. He sat me and Charlie down at the table. He told me I could stay there, but there'd be rules. Charlie and I needed to stay out of trouble, and I would have to earn my keep. Mr. Carpenter owned a drugstore in town. I was to go to work with him every day and help out at the store."

"Let's see how things go in a week or two."

"Yes, sir," I said.

"And, Patrick, I'm really sorry this has happened to you. I know you're a good kid," he said, and I could tell from the look on his face he meant it.

"Thank you, Mr. Carpenter," I said, trying not to get choked up again.

It was time to call Janet. I needed to tell her where I was and what had happened. Luckily, Phil wasn't there when she answered. After filling her in she said, "Oh, Patrick, I'm so sorry. Dad's got a horrible temper, that's for sure, but he'll get over it. You'll be able to go back home."

"No," I said.

"No, what?"

"No I don't think he'll get over it, and no I don't want to ever go back home."

"Patrick, you can't mean that."

"I do mean it. I swear I'd just shrivel up and die if I lived there. Somehow I'll get through this. I just wanted you to know where I was."

"I wish you could come live with me…"

"That's not why I called. I know you don't have room for me and that's okay." Janet and Phil were crammed into a tiny apartment. Besides, Janet was expecting her first baby in November. They had neither the space nor the extra money to take me in.

"The Carpenters have been really good to me, so don't worry."

"I know them and I'm glad they're letting you stay. Please, Patrick, keep letting me know how you're doing? Promise?"

I promised and hung up.

Surprisingly the work at the drugstore turned out to be something I enjoyed. I liked the different people that came in; helping them find things they needed, keeping the shelves stocked, mopping, and helping close up the store at night. And when things were slow, Mr. Carpenter and I talked. I'd never had an adult listen to me like that before. I told him about my mother and how much I missed her. I explained my love of writing and my dream of becoming a journalist.

For a while I went out with Charlie at night. He worked for a construction company and had gotten quite tan and muscular. That along with his blond hair and blue eyes made him quite the ladies' man. But I soon grew tired of partying and insisted we get home at a decent hour, which ticked him off. I didn't want to rock the boat with his parents. I needed to keep on their good side.

It wasn't long before Charlie bought himself a Harley. He could be heard roaring in on his motorcycle in the wee hours of the morning. I didn't know how he could keep going like that, keeping such late hours and continuing to get up to go to work every day. After a couple weeks he stopped asking me to go with him at all. He told me I wasn't fun anymore. I could feel our friendship slipping away.

Mrs. Carpenter was never really happy with me staying there, though she always treated me kindly. I think she just wasn't sure it was right. I should be living with my father. I tried to show my appreciation by offering to help with dishes, or weeding her garden, but she always turned down my offers. At least she knew I wasn't just some kid looking for a free handout.

Charlie began to act differently towards me. At dinner his dad and I would often relate stories about things that had happened at work. We had a laugh at forgetful Mrs. Morehouse who had stood at the counter for ten minutes trying to remember why she'd come into the store, chatting away until finally giving up and buying something she didn't need, just so as not to have wasted a trip; then there was Mr. Flannery who forgot to put his teeth in that morning, making it difficult to understand what he was asking; and Mrs. Slater with her active five year old twins who got into everything. Mostly candy. The whole time Charlie sulked.

I made sure to ask him about his day. He offered little comment in response. It was obvious he had become jealous of me when one day he said, "I'm sick of you always kissing up to my parents." I told him I was just trying to let them know how much I appreciated being able to stay there. He began to spend less and less time with me. Sometimes he didn't even come home for dinner. As an only child, Charlie never liked sharing—even if it was with his best friend.

As fall approached I started thinking hard about finding a new place to live. Taking Mr. Carpenter's advice I had enrolled in two classes at the community college in Muskegon. Mr. Carpenter said he would make sure I had a ride to get there. I'd been assigned a guidance counselor, whom I'd never met, to help me plan my curriculum. I took a gamble and made an appointment; maybe my advisor could help me sort everything out. I borrowed Mrs. Carpenter's car and drove to Muskegon to meet with her.

As I walked into the counselor's office I was so nervous I could hardly sit. My money would run out soon and I wouldn't be able to afford any more classes. I didn't want to impose on Mr. and Mrs. Carpenter any longer. Maybe I should just skip going to college altogether and get a job like Charlie. Even so, doing that and affording a place to live would take some time.

Grace Winslow was a woman of about sixty with straight steel-gray hair down to her shoulders, which she parted in the middle. Perched on her nose sat a pair of black-rimmed reading glasses; when removed they revealed calm blue eyes the color of robin's eggs. Putting down her glasses she asked, "What can I do for you, Mr. Crabtree?"

That always threw me off balance—Mr. Crabtree was my father—but here at college every student was addressed by his or her last name. It felt so...adult, and I didn't feel much like an adult as yet.

I took a deep breath and told her everything I felt important. She listened without saying a word or even nodding her head. Did she think I was overstating my circumstances? Was I just a spoiled young adult whining about how hard life was now that I was out on my own?

When I finished and leaned back in the chair I realized I'd been sitting on the edge of the seat, my hands tightly gripping the arms, every muscle in my body taunt with the stress of the situation.

"Mr. Crabtree, may I call you Patrick?" I nodded. "You're in quite a difficult situation. I've looked into your high school grades. You were a good student. Very active in school activities, as well. What is it you hope to do?"

"I want to be a journalist," I replied.

She nodded. "I see you've signed up for an English class and a creative writing class. Do you like to read?"

"Yes, I read a lot—when I can find the time, that is."

"Good. I've always found that people who read a lot make better writers." She leaned back in her chair and tapped a pencil on the top of her desk. Finally she said, "Give me a week, Patrick, to see if I can do anything to help your situation."

So I left, not knowing if I'd made any progress or not.

I worried all week. I tried not to mope as I worked around the drugstore, but if this didn't work out, what was I going to do? Nervously, I borrowed the car again to meet Mrs. Winslow the following week. I thought I saw a slight smile on her face when I entered her office.

Mrs. Winslow said she had talked to Reverend Hartwick. He and his wife rented rooms to college students. They provided one meal per day. I started to interrupt, telling her I had no way to pay for a room, when she held up her hand.

"Let me finish, Patrick," she said. So I sat there listening to the plan she laid out. If I needed work, there was a job available in the evenings at the college cleaning offices. It would provide enough money for my room and board and allow me to save for more classes. There was also a scholarship available that she was quite sure I could get.

Instantly my body registered relief; the stress seemed to drain right out of me. I felt tears sting my eyes wondering if I'd been saved at last. I vowed to do anything they asked me to do to make this work.

Later that week I moved into the Reverend's home. They rented to two other students and over time other students came and went; but I stayed—taking classes part time and working—for three years.

My days were usually spent going to classes in the morning, studying in the afternoon, and then dinner with the Reverend and his wife. Afterwards I'd be off to my cleaning job. Along about midnight

I'd return to my room where I often continued to study. I was content. I liked having a routine and being responsible only for myself. There was a lot less stress in my life.

In my third year I met Nora.

20

I actually already knew Nora Troyer, but not well. She had been two years behind me in high school. I was sitting on my usual bench in the park next to the administration building reading an assignment, when I saw her go past the first time. She was walking a little black cocker spaniel. Well, trying to at least. The dog was having trouble sniffing and walking at the same time because its ears kept getting in the way. She didn't appear to notice me, so I made no attempt to say hello. But Nora never missed anything; even seeming not to see me, she had.

The next day she passed by again, and took interest in something on the other side of the park, never looking my way. Oh well, I thought. Maybe she doesn't remember me. Not that she should.

On Wednesday after walking past me, she suddenly turned towards me and said, "You're Patrick Crabtree, aren't you?" Every day during her lunch hour, Nora walked their dog, Spanky. She said she'd noticed me sitting there and thought I most certainly looked like Patrick Crabtree, so she decided to stop and say hello. With that she sat down next to me, her plump little dog settling down by my feet, panting as if it had just completed a doggy marathon

Nora wore her blond hair cut shorter now, soft loose curls accentuating hazel eyes. She had a scattering of freckles across her nose (which I was later to learn she hated passionately). I thought she looked adorable. I hadn't had much luck with girls—too much baggage on my part—so I'd let her do most of the talking, not wanting to make a fool of myself.

As she talked I learned she no longer lived in Brooks Creek. Her parents had divorced, and she and her mother moved to a small house close to the college. Her mother worked there in admissions and Nora worked as a secretary. Her older brother, Jack, had moved to Chicago to be with her dad. Mr. Troyer owned an insurance company where Jack also worked.

I told her I was a student, but also cleaned offices at night, including the one she worked in. Nora thought it interesting that our paths had crossed like that. I didn't know about interesting, but at least she didn't turn her nose up at my janitorial job.

Thursday I sat on the same park bench hoping she might pass by again, but she didn't. I was disappointed. What had I expected? Did I really have anything to offer someone like Nora? She made me realize how much I'd missed having someone to talk to, and it didn't hurt that Nora was very attractive. I told myself she had just been friendly, no more than that. She was probably avoiding me, not wanting to give the impression that she was interested in me.

Still, I couldn't get her out of my mind as I cleaned that night. After several offices, I finally came to hers. I began moving chairs so I could vacuum the carpet when I saw a folded piece of paper taped to the top of a wastebasket with my name on it. In her neat handwriting she had written, "Meet me tomorrow for coffee at McDonald's. I get off work at five. Nora."

The next morning getting ready for classes, I dressed much more carefully than I normally did—put on my least worn-looking pants, and a freshly laundered shirt. The day passed slowly. I had a hard time keeping my mind on the instructor. I kept telling myself this was just a visit over coffee with someone from my home town. No big deal. By five o'clock I was so convinced she wouldn't show that I'd taken a book along with me to read. When I saw her sitting at a little table with her back to me, I almost turned around and left. She couldn't possibly be waiting for me—but then she turned and smiled.

I'd told Mrs. Hartwick I wouldn't be home for dinner that night. If we were having a good conversation, I didn't want to suddenly have to get up and leave. Nora was easy to talk to. She didn't ask many personal questions, not then anyway, and seemed genuinely interested in my college plans. After an hour we decided to order burgers and fries. While we ate I told her about the other guys renting rooms at the Hartwick's, like the one who always left a mess in the bathroom we shared. I finally got sick of telling him to clean up and decided to booby trap the medicine cabinet. When he opened the cabinet door one morning, a barrage of ping-pong balls fell out and bounced around the bathroom. I liked that I could make her laugh. She had a beautiful smile, the kind that made you want to smile in return.

Still, I was cautious. I tried to avoid entanglements. I didn't even hang out with other guys from college or those who roomed at the Hartwick's. There wasn't a lot of extra time in my life, and I didn't need any distractions from my studies. I had become a different person, no longer the sociable outgoing kid from high school.

But over the months our friendship grew and developed into a much more serious relationship. Though I was on a limited budget, we often caught a movie or stopped for pizza and a beer. I'd bought a beat up Volkswagen by then that barely held together, but it got me to where I needed to go.

When I met Mrs. Troyer, Nora's mother, I liked her immediately. She was just an older version of Nora—always smiling, full of enthusiasm, and seemed untarnished by her divorce. She loved to travel, and was saving up for a trip to Europe. She also seemed to genuinely like me, which was a plus.

Nora often asked to meet my dad, but I refused. She seemed to think that all it would take was a visit to resolve our issues. But she couldn't have been more wrong, and I knew it. I wasn't ready to see him yet.

Buddy was the one friend with whom I still had contact. One night when I was talking to him on the phone, telling him about a good movie Nora and I had just seen, he said, "Kaitlyn and I are on the outs again."

Kaitlyn, was his on-and-off again girlfriend, who for the last year and a half had left him for other guys several times, then when it didn't work out would come back wanting to pick up where they'd left off. She was quite spoiled in my opinion, but Buddy seemed pretty stuck on her.

"I'm sick of all the drama," he said.

"Well, you've certainly given her enough time to make up her mind. I hate to say it Buddy, but—"

"I know, she's just using me until she finds someone with more money, more—"

"Forget Kaitlyn! I've got the perfect girl for you."

"Man, you're not giving up, Nora, are you?" he said with a laugh. Buddy had met Nora a few times and always said he'd wished he'd met her before I did. I reminded him he had gone to the same high school I had, so he'd had plenty of chances.

"Absolutely not. But she has a friend—"

"Oh, no, I can see where this is going. I'm not getting fixed up with somebody. I'm not that desperate."

"Look, just meet her. She's almost as beautiful as Nora," I said, smiling to myself, "and just as smart. I think you'd really hit it off."

It took a lot of convincing, but he finally agreed to one date to check Sarah out. Well, she'd be checking him out, too. We arranged to meet up the following Saturday to take in a movie, then go to Fricano's for pizza.

We ended up laughing and talking until the bar closed. It was the one and only time I'd ever played matchmaker for anyone, but it worked out incredibly well. Soon our foursome could be seen together most weekends, as both of our relationships grew. I had both my beautiful Nora and my best friend in my life. I couldn't have been happier.

As I came to the end of my third year, Nora and I had been dating seriously for about a year. I'd gone as far as I could at the community college. It was time to transfer to a four year university. Money again became a worry—as was relocating, finding a job, affordable housing, and leaving behind the friendships I had come to enjoy. And of course, I especially worried how my relationship with Nora would work out.

Nora and I had talked about getting married in the future, but the future was murky. She began pushing for us to get married right away and move to Chicago to be near her father. She had talked to him, unbeknown to me, about offering me a job. He said he would be willing to train me for a position in his insurance office. Nora insisted that with my salary and hers, when she found a job, we'd be able to live on our own.

I was back to a stress level I hadn't felt in a long time. Everything was moving too fast. I was getting those all too familiar knots in my stomach. I couldn't eat; sleep was near impossible. I didn't want to quit working towards my degree, not after getting this far, but the thought of losing Nora was too much. I'd finally found someone I cared about who cared about me in return. She assured me I could work and still take classes at night. It would take longer, but it was still possible for me to finish. Deep down I didn't believe that would ever happen, but I so much wanted it to be true, I finally agreed to her plans. Putting aside my reservations, I threw myself into wedding plans and the move to Chicago.

Nora and I were married in June by Reverend Hartwick. Buddy was my best man and Sarah was the maid of honor. Janet and her family came, but though dad had been sent an invitation, he didn't come. The one I really missed was Charlie. I sure wished he had been there.

At the reception, which was a small affair held in the basement of the church where wedding cake and coffee was served, Janet handed me an envelope. It was from dad. There was nothing written on the front. Inside, no card or note; just a check made out for one hundred dollars. I wasn't sure what to make of it.

It had been three years since I'd last seen my father, the day of our fight over college. Nora was insistent that this was an offering of truce. She said we needed to stop at the farm on our way back from our honeymoon at Mackinac Island. I balked at the idea. But Nora, once her mind was made up, would not back down. So I asked Janet to let dad know we might stop by. That way it wouldn't come as a complete surprise.

I was sweating the afternoon we entered dad's driveway, even though the day was unusually chilly. I was worried about what he might say about me in front of Nora and how I would respond. But I needn't have worried. He mostly ignored me. I was treated more like an acquaintance than a son.

As Nora chatted him up, he even smiled a couple times. I tried to think of things to say, but everything seemed so insignificant, so I said little. Back on the road to Chicago she said, "Well, he's not so bad, Patrick. I was really expecting an ogre of some kind. Are you sure you didn't make him out to be worse than he is?"

I didn't answer. I had no words.

After we moved to Chicago, we still visited Michigan often. We were there for her mother's fiftieth birthday, and her grandmother's eightieth. We spent a week camping near Sleeping Bear Dunes. For weeks afterwards we found beach sand in our car. The next summer we followed the Leelanau Peninsula Wine Trail, tasting fine wines of northern Michigan. We brought several bottles back with us to savor over the winter, reminding ourselves of our time sitting at little tables sipping wine as we looked at the sparkling waters of Lake Michigan. Each time on our way home, Nora insisted we stop and see dad. She seemed to think if we made enough stops, some day we would reach the point where the relationship would thaw and we would all live happily ever after. But each time we stopped, he put all his attention on Nora, and I was pretty much invisible.

Two years into our marriage we were back in Michigan for Buddy and Sarah's wedding. This time I was best man and Nora maid of honor. In a shimmering, strapless dress of teal green, Nora looked more beautiful than ever. We danced into the night with my arm around her waist, her head on my shoulder. I breathed in the sweet fragrance of her hair and asked myself, how had I ended up so lucky?

21

Once settled in Chicago and working for Nora's father it was quickly confirmed there would be no time for night classes. The hours at the insurance office were long and Nora's dad, Jack Sr., was a task master of unrelenting demands. Everything I did was scrutinized—every i dotted, every t crossed. I don't think it helped that I was his son-in-law. He wanted to make sure no one in the office thought I was getting preferential treatment. But I'd learned one thing from my father early on; do it right the first time. Even though Jack's strict running of the office back then often exasperated me, he helped me become quite proficient at what I do, and successful enough that I don't have to worry about paying my bills.

Even with my chances of working on my degree evaporating, I was still happy. Nora and I lived in a small apartment and with little to do on weekends we took to exploring our new home. Neither one of us had ever lived in a large city. We were overwhelmed by the sheer size of it; the buildings, the traffic, the noise, and the amount of people rushing everywhere. The city was alive and full of excitement.

One Saturday we spent hours exploring the Field Museum of Natural History. As we wandered through ancient artifact collections and cultural exhibits from around the world, I couldn't help but wish

Janet was with us to see it all. A few weeks later we made our way to the Shedd Aquarium where we laughed at the antics of otters and penguins, and were amazed by the size of beluga whales.

We both took the day off on our first St. Patrick's Day so we could watch the parade. We shook our heads at the Chicago River dyed dark green, and drank green beer from frosty mugs at a local pub.

And when it was Nora's birthday I took her to the Chicago Institute of Art. There we viewed exhibits and paintings done by famous people I'd only heard of, but knew nothing about. Afterwards we had a leisurely lunch at the Walnut Room, an elegant restaurant on the seventh floor of Macy's. We'd sat admiring the beautiful wood paneling imported from Russia and the Austrian chandeliers, all the while sipping wine and dining on their famous Chicken Pot Pie.

Coming from such a rural background we felt as if we'd moved to another country, rather than from just across lake.

Several weekends on hot summer days Nora's dad would take us out on his sailboat on Lake Michigan where we rode the waves and stared at blue skies for miles. I took to sailing right away. Jack taught me how to set sail, trim fore and aft, and how to tack. By the end of the first summer, Jack declared me a born sailor.

Nora's enthusiasm for any new adventure was contagious and I looked forward to every moment we could spend together. Even though I disliked my job, the weekends with Nora made up for it. I hoped things would never change.

On Sundays in the summer Nora and I often strolled down the River Walk hand in hand. We'd find a small table and sit sipping lattes. While Nora skimmed the Sunday Chicago Tribune, I read a book I'd brought along. We'd 'people watch' at the same time often commenting on the stranger ones—and believe me there was no shortage of strange people in Chicago. Unfortunately every year when fall came along we had to give up this cherished Sunday habit until the warmth of spring returned.

On one of these Sunday mornings I looked over at Nora frowning at something on the Style page and thought how stunning she always looked. Her designer sunglasses were pushed up on her head where they sat on soft blond curls. She was wearing white linen shorts which contrasted nicely with her tan legs, crossed at the knee, one foot continually bouncing up and down in a slow rhythm. A sleeveless apricot top showed off her well-toned arms from daily gym workouts; surrounding her neck a chiffon scarf with orange, turquoise, and yellow swirls lay across her shoulders. Every time she moved her head the golden hoops dangling from her ears gave off glints of sunlight

I couldn't take my eyes off my beautiful wife.

"It's time, Patrick," she said.

"Time for what?" I asked, suddenly startled out of my thoughts.

"Time for a baby."

Well, that was Nora. She never believed in easing into a conversation. One of the things I liked about Nora was you always knew what she was thinking; one of the things I disliked about Nora was you always knew what she was thinking.

I sucked in air while I tried to figure out the best response. This statement was quite unexpected, though upon reflection, it shouldn't have been. Her brother Jack and his wife Karen had just had their first child, a little boy they named Justin.

"We've been married three years, Patrick. It's time to move to the next step, don't you agree? You do want a family, don't you?"

Truth was, I loved it just being the two of us, but I could see the hope in her eyes.

"Of course, Nora," I said, "You just caught me by surprise, is all."

"And we need to start looking for a house."

"Leave our little apartment? I thought you liked it there."

"I do, Patrick. But the key word is 'little'. There's no room for a baby and I'm not going to carry all that baby stuff up and down three flights of stairs."

"Isn't this a bit premature—I mean, you aren't even pregnant yet." Then a thought hit me and I added, "Are you?"

"No, no Patrick, I'm not, but it takes time to find a house, and I'm not going to get involved in moving while I'm pregnant."

Her mind was made up. We started looking for a house. Let's just say, I was less than enthusiastic. Every weekend for the next three months, we looked at property. Nora knew exactly what she wanted, of course. I would've settled for many of the houses we looked at, but she rejected them all.

Our house would have to have two bathrooms, at least three bedrooms, one of which needed to be the perfect room for a nursery. A first floor laundry was a must, and she wanted an open kitchen so that she would be able to keep an eye on our child when she was busy making dinner. There needed to be a fenced in yard on a street that had very little traffic. The local schools had to be top notch.

Every Monday I went back to work thinking how much I missed our old weekends together.

When we finally settled on a house, which was way more than I had hoped to spend, that was just the beginning. Nora insisted every room had to be painted, with special care for the room that would be a nursery. Finally she decided on yellow, as we didn't know whether we would have a boy or girl, so the color could work well for either.

The yard needed some updating; old shrubs pulled out and new ones planted. We had someone come in and trim trees so that no big limbs would fall into the yard and hurt the baby. When a neighbor had a swing set up for sale we bought it and spent an entire weekend getting it from their house to ours. It was all getting a bit insane.

But it was worse than that. After a year of no baby, Nora began talking about one as if it was just over the horizon. She began buying baby things and storing them in the nursery; a changing table—the sale price too good to pass up, a stroller, a crib that could be turned into a bed as the child got older, and lots of baby clothes in various sizes, taking care that they could be used for either a girl or boy. She would show me her new purchases and ask, "Isn't this just adorable?"

Friends would often ask about the baby; when was it due? Nora would answer evasively saying, "Oh, it can't come any too soon," then smile and pat her tummy.

After a while though, people began to get suspicious and soon avoided the topic completely. As time went on, her friends stopped hanging out with us. They were getting uncomfortable feelings about Nora and the baby. I was getting quite uncomfortable myself wondering where this was going to go if she didn't get pregnant soon.

Three years after moving into the 'baby house', as I secretly called it, we were sitting on worn, cushioned chairs in Dr. Hamilton's office, my sweaty hands sticking to the wooden arms. Dr. Hamilton was the doctor Nora had been seeing for some time now. He was supposedly going to help her get to the bottom of the no-baby problem, and once they knew what to do, well, then, it would only be a matter of time. Nora had undergone more tests and today we would get the results. I was sick of sitting in those chairs. Time after time, nothing good had ever come from it.

Dr. Hamilton came into the room and sat down behind his desk, laying a file down in front of him, which he never opened. His expression gave nothing away. But it wasn't long before we realized the news was devastating. Nora was physically unable to have children and nothing could be done to change that. He rattled off test results in a tone someone might have used to read a grocery list. He cut Nora into little pieces. One test at a time. I have no idea if he knew he was hurting her so much. Maybe he'd found there was no easier way to say what he had to say other than to bluntly tell us there was no way we could ever have a child, then send us out of his office as quickly as possible.

As Dr. Hamilton began babbling something about adoption, Nora stood up. Without saying a word she opened the door and left the room. I followed behind her, not knowing what to say. Her calmness scared the hell out of me.

"Nora," I started to say once we were out of the building.

She raised her hand to my face. "Not now, Patrick!"

No tears. I would've given anything for tears.

I looked into her eyes then and saw something I'd only seen before in my own mirror. I was no stranger to the disappointment I saw there. Deep disappointment. The kind that sucks you down into a hole so deep you're certain you'll never see daylight again.

I realized something then about Nora. Nora had never known disappointment. Not the all-encompassing despair I'd lived through. Nora had lived a charmed life. She had always envisioned life on her own terms. Once her mind was made up, she laid out her plans, and then proceeded to get what she wanted.

Chapter 21

Nothing had prepared Nora for this.

22

Over weeks and months despair turned into anger, anger into rage. There was nothing that could be said. I could only hope that in time Nora would be able to come to terms with her grief, for grief is what it was—grief over losing a child she'd never had. I loved her more than ever. Nothing would change that. It hurt to see her so distraught. But all attempts on my part to help her were met with stony silence or anger so extreme I had to leave the house for hours to let her vent. The door to the nursery was closed the day we returned from Dr. Hamilton's office. To my knowledge she never went in there again. I wanted to get rid of the baby things, but I couldn't bring myself to even suggest it.

One day when I had been trying unsuccessfully to lift her spirits, I told her we knew other couples who didn't have children, and yet they were able to go on and have happy lives together.

She erupted, like a volcano long over-due.

"You never wanted to be a father. I knew it! I knew it all along! You were just humoring me."

It was true, I was uneasy about being a father. I wasn't sure I'd make a good one since my own father had been such a horrible role model, but I often thought about what it would be like to teach a son how to ride a bike, take him fishing, or watch him hit a ball at a Little League game. I had more trouble picturing a daughter, but I'd have loved any child, boy or girl. Her accusation was unfair. But she was full of anger and that anger had to go somewhere.

Another late afternoon I came in from mowing the lawn and saw Nora preparing dinner in the kitchen. It would be another dinner eaten in silence. It reminded me of the dinners I'd eaten with my father after my mother died. The long silences and the uncomfortable tension. I so missed the long conversations we used to have. We seldom had company anymore. Most of our friends found Nora's anger, even when she tried to cover it up with false gaiety, too toxic. Like me, they ran out of things to say.

I'd been thinking of something one Saturday afternoon and broached the subject carefully, trying not to start another fight. "Nora, tomorrow's Sunday. Why don't we drive into the city and go to The River Walk, get a latte and read the paper? Do some 'people watching? We haven't done that in a long time. I've missed that, haven't you?"

"I'm not interested in watching a bunch of weirdos," she said sarcastically as she continued chopping vegetables for a salad.

"Really Nora, it might be nice to have a change of scenery for a day."

Chop, chop, chop. No response. Her mind was made up as usual. Made up to not allow herself, or me either for that matter, to try to go on with life.

A few weeks later I suggested we sell the house and move back to the city. I did my best to sound upbeat. "We could find another apartment, Nora. We were happy there."

Chapter 22

Again I was met with anger, this time worse than most. "Yes, let's just pretend none of this has happened. Just turn back the clock, right, Patrick? You think that will solve everything, don't you? Well, it won't work!"

"What will?" I pleaded. But she had no answer. Instead she threw the glass of water she had been holding into the sink where it shattered, and left the room sobbing.

I begged her to go to counseling. I promised to go with her. I suggested talking to Reverend Hartwick. I told her I'd do whatever she wanted. She just had to tell me what that was.

But, the truth was, she didn't have an answer to give me. And I was out of ideas. She had closed the door on our marriage the same way she closed it on the nursery, never to be opened again.

Finally, we came to a truce of sorts. Babies were never mentioned. Neither was moving. The job I hated became my safe haven. I started dreading weekends. My life had turned upside down.

As for Nora, she seemed to always have somewhere to go when she wasn't at work. She moved into the guest bedroom. We'd become strangers.

It was our seventh wedding anniversary. I'd stopped and picked up flowers and headed home, wondering if I could convince her to go out for dinner. She met me in the kitchen. I knew something had changed. There was a resolve in her eyes I'd not seen before. Almost in the same breath, she told me Sarah and Buddy had just had their baby, a little girl—and she wanted a divorce.

The impact of those words, "I want a divorce," hit me so hard I fell back against the cupboard. I'd never given up hope that someday things between us would be good again, unlikely as that may have seemed, but her look was cold and fixed. All signs of my Nora were gone. She had just kept disintegrating until finally nothing I recognized was left.

I spent two hours pleading, telling her I loved her, reminding her of all the love we had for each other when we were first married. That not having a baby was no one's fault. It had been out of our control. I told her I was willing to do anything. But her mind was made up. She had already packed her bags. They were in her car. She was going to stay with her mother.

After the divorce I went through the motions of living. Nora's brother, Jack, now my boss, never gave me any hassle over the divorce as he and his wife had split up the year before. He knew too well how relationships could go wrong.

I continued to do ordinary things. I'd go to work, grocery shop, and do my laundry. Now and then I'd go out with the guys from work for a drink. Mostly I buried myself in writing. It was the only time I felt any peace. If I wasn't writing, I was thinking about writing. It's how I'd survived.

As for my dad, I still saw him from time to time. He never asked where Nora was. I don't know if he knew about the divorce or not, but I'm sure he suspected. He'd probably added that to my list of failures.

Two years after our divorce was final, Nora married again. This time to a man much older than her, widowed, with two children.

23

Dolly got up and stretched. She came over and began doing a little dance in front of me.

"Do you need to go out, girl?" I asked, getting up. As I made my way to the door I tried to remember if I'd fed her that evening.

I was a bit unsteady on my feet. I'd been sitting there drinking and reliving memories for hours. What was the point of going through all this pain again? Whenever I allowed myself to think about the past, I ended up depressed for weeks. Yet I couldn't seem to stop myself. This wasn't how I wanted to live the rest of my life, stuck in the past, wanting a life I could never have.

I let Dolly out into the yard and waited for her to finish. When she came back in she headed to the stairs. Half way up she turned and looked at me over her shoulder.

"No, Dolly, I'm not ready to go to bed yet," I said, carefully making my way back to the chair. I knew there was no way I could sleep. Dolly came over and dropped down next to me with a sigh. I topped up my drink and took a sip.

The room seemed to have grown smaller since darkness set in. I reached over and switched on the lamp. Shadows appeared on the walls. The loose bulb made them flicker and dance over the old wallpaper. I didn't like the way they lurched at me, coming closer, then fading back. They reminded me too much of ghosts. Who knows; maybe they were ghosts. There sure had been enough of them to go around the last few days.

As I settled in the chair a chill began to creep up my spine to the back of my neck. I reached over and pulled an old afghan off the couch and wrapped it around me. It was something my mother had crocheted many years ago.

The full moon peaked out from behind the clouds. Cast shadows from the maple tree spread across the walls. Their leaf-shaped hands moved with the wind; gnarled fingers stretched towards me. All the air seemed sucked out of the room.

My skin began to tingle.

I needed to stop; to think about something besides ghosts.

I sat up straighter and began to study the wallpaper. How long had it been there I wondered? It was probably something my Grandmother Crabtree had put up years ago. It was dirty and yellowed. In many places it had become loose at the seams and at the ceiling. The paper seemed to be struggling to free itself from the walls.

I thought of my mother sitting in this room at night, poetry book in her lap. When she stared at the lines of gray-green vines that climbed up the wallpaper from floor to ceiling, had she felt imprisoned by them; imprisoned by the choices she'd made?

A sudden breeze from the open window began rifling the pages of the book I'd left open on the table next to me. Dolly stirred, then settled back down.

I turned back to the wallpaper again. Once vibrant pink roses had lost most of their color; their edges blurred as they faded into the background, making me think of the thin, pale-pink color of blood in water. After all, I'd been sitting there all night ripping scabs off wounds, leaving them open and ugly. My thoughts had left me bruised and bloodied.

Outside the wind was blowing harder. Leaves swirled around the yard; branches crashed against the sides of the house. I heard the banging door of the chicken coop that had been left unlatched. From behind the barn came the barks of coyotes on the hunt.

Inside the murmurings in the room continued to grow louder. I tried to ignore them, not wanting to acknowledge their presence. But there *were* ghosts and I had unleashed them. It was too late.

They had become menacing, circling me shark-like. I was their prey and they were hungry. The voices had tormented me all night, and I could do little to resist them. Finally, I was too exhausted to fight them off any longer. I drew the blanket tightly around me, gathering courage from it. Quietly I waited.

I didn't have to wait long.

You don't need no college education to run a farm...

Dad's voice, of course. Dead and buried, he still wasn't done with me yet. I wasn't surprised my father had something to say. He knew I'd never gotten that degree, and he wasn't going to let me forget it. Well, it was his turn to listen. There were things I'd needed to say to him for years. And I was going to say them.

I leaned forward, staring into the face I could not see. "I'd never planned on running a farm. That was your plan, remember? You never asked me what I wanted out of life, and even after you knew, it didn't matter. You were too intent on laying out my life for me instead. Did it surprise you that I just didn't lay down and let you walk all over me?"

You're not doing it on my money.

"Well, I didn't need your money," I said, picking up my glass and taking another drink. "I went to college on money I earned. I worked for every penny. After the night I left, I never asked you for anything again my whole life. You could have helped, but instead you turned your back on me, like you always did. I did it all without you. Your precious money meant nothing to me."

Still he wasn't ready to let me go.

"You're only worth half a person as it is..."

I slammed the glass down. "You couldn't even call me a man, could you? No, to you I'd always be a little boy. Someone you could bully into being your hired-hand. But you did me a favor the way I look at it. I may not have become a journalist, but there's no shame in what I've done with my life."

He was like a dog with a bone. He just wasn't going to release me.

You're not staying here with all your high-minded ideas.

"Those high-minded ideas, as you called them, were just my way of trying to prepare myself for the future. What was so wrong with that? Is it written in stone somewhere that sons have to have the same occupation as their fathers? Leaving was the best thing I ever did. All I lost was a father I never had. But you, you lost your son."

I leaned back in my chair. I reached over and tried to tighten the lightbulb to stop the shadows from moving, but it resisted my efforts. I should've gotten up then and left the room, but I seemed trapped in my chair, a prisoner to his voice, the walls pressing in.

...whispering about my son the thief?

That was it. He'd finally done it. He'd crossed the line. I could take no more as I leapt out of my chair screaming at the unfairness of it all. All the anger and disappointment, the feelings of being abandoned I'd felt for years came pouring out in a fury. Grabbing my glass I threw it across the room. It smashed against the wall causing glistening shards to fall to the floor leaving behind streams of whiskey to trickle down the wallpaper.

Dolly scrambled to her feet. Cowering the whole way, she ran out of the room and found refuge beneath the kitchen table.

"My, God!" I yelled. "You've dumped all that guilt on me for years! That's the only time I've ever really done anything wrong. But there's never any forgiveness for wrongs done, is there? No, you were more worried about what people might say than to be proud of me for graduating."

I stopped and began taking in deep breaths; then, trembling I sat back down on the edge of my chair, trying to pull myself together.

"But how about you, Dad? Should I forgive you? It works both ways, doesn't it? I admitted my mistake and worked to make things right, but what have you done? Tell me, what have you ever done for any of us? You were never man enough to own up to your own mistakes, or to say you were sorry. Maybe you never felt you'd committed any wrongs, but either way, my slate is clean. You can't hold that mistake over me anymore. I'm a good person and no one can say any different."

I paused for a moment, still shaking. Finally, I added, "And while I'm at it, I'm sick and tired of feeling guilty for wanting to live my own life. I've nothing to feel guilty about. It's not selfish to want something different. I've made the right choices. I'm my own person.

And I'll never have to come to this house again to try and win your love. All those times I came to see you, you never once made any effort to work things out between us. Now it's too late. But that was your choice, not mine. Maybe you couldn't forgive me for leaving, but you'd left me long before that."

Done, I slumped back in the chair. I'd said my piece. Relieved, I'd felt him leave.

But now I was beginning to feel sick. I knew better than to drink on an empty stomach. Hours ago I should've gotten up and found something to eat, but that had seemed like too much effort. I got up and went to the kitchen intent on getting something from the refrigerator, but returned instead with another empty glass. After filling it, I sat back down, hoping I didn't have to listen to any more voices.

But then the flickering light worsened.

You never wanted a baby. I knew it! You were just humoring me.

"So you're here, too, Nora?" I sighed. "Well, I'm not surprised. But you're wrong. I did want a baby. What I didn't want was to be blamed for something over which I'd no control. You just decided to stop living your life. You liked the role of victim too much. There was nothing I was ever going to do or say that would let me off the hook as the guilty person in our marriage.

But guilty of what, I never really knew. Maybe you thought I wasn't suffering enough. You certainly could out-suffer me. Was this just some kind of contest over who had been hurt the most?

Whatever it was, it was a role I never wanted. You hung that on me and wouldn't let go no matter how much I tried to love you. You thought you were the only one hurt by not being able to have a child, thinking only you could feel pain, that by loving me you'd have to give up all those feelings of anger that you so cherished. But I had felt hurt and disappointment, too.

The difference was you had someone who loved you, no matter what. Your love for me came with conditions. You threw it all away, Nora."

The clouds began to cover the moon again. The shadows fading. Everything seemed to settle down, to be less threatening. Maybe they were all leaving. They'd found out I wasn't as easy to intimidate as they'd thought.

I shook my head. I must be losing my mind. I needed get up now and go to bed—get out of that damn room. I started to rise...

But then, there was still someone else left in the room. I could feel it.

You're just not fun anymore.

"Charlie, no! Please, God, not Charlie, too," I pleaded. "Don't make me remember! It's too much!"

But I couldn't stop.

I'd heard the pain in Mr. Carpenter's voice when he called me that Sunday morning. I had been living with the Hartwicks for about a year, but I often stopped in to see Mr. Carpenter. He was my mentor and my friend.

He told me he had lain awake every night until he heard the sound of Charlie's motorcycle on the gravel as he came up the driveway. Then he would hear the engine shut off, and Charlie's footsteps as he came up the steps to his bedroom. Once he knew Charlie was safely in his room, he could finally relax and go to sleep.

But that morning at three a.m. Charlie still wasn't home. Mr. Carpenter had tossed and turned. Finally, he'd gotten up and gone downstairs to sit in his TV chair to wait. This time he and Charlie were going to have a talk. He was going to lay the law down. He couldn't keep worrying like this every night.

By five a.m. he was sure Charlie had either been arrested, or God forbid, was in a hospital somewhere. He had prayed all night for him to be okay and get back home safely.

But hope soon faded when lights came up the driveway and he knew they weren't from Charlie's motorcycle. A state police cruiser pulled up to the front door and two officers got out. The looks on their faces told him everything. Hats in hand, the officers made their way to the door and told him what had happened.

Charlie had left The Driftwood Bar around two a.m. He'd had an altercation with another young man over Andrea, the woman he'd been dating. When he left the bar, she refused to go with him.

"Thank God, for that," I remembered Mr. Carpenter saying.

Charlie had been traveling at a high rate of speed down River Road when he failed to negotiate a curve and hit a large oak tree head on. He died at the scene before the emergency vehicles were able to get to him.

I'd felt Charlie's death deeply. Even all these years later I still felt such loss when I thought about him. I'd always regretted not keeping in touch with him like I had with Buddy. But Charlie and I didn't have the same relationship anymore. We no longer had anything in common. I didn't like all the partying and he thought I was too serious. I wasn't the fun loving kid I'd been back when we were in school. But I still missed him—his wise cracking ways, his need for adventure, his loyalty to both Buddy and me as we went through adolescence together.

Chapter 23

The voices had stopped. There was a stillness in the room broken only by the sound of someone softly crying. Then I realized it was me.

"Charlie," I wept, "my friend, my friend..."

24

I rubbed my eyes with the backs of my hands. I was out of tears. I was hollowed out. I sat there limp, only bone and flesh holding me together. I was like the ghosts; shadowy, empty, devoid of all feeling, swirling around in a milieu of darkness. Maybe I had become one.

Dolly had returned to the doorway. She sat watching me intently as I picked up my glass to take another drink and stared dully at the wall opposite me with all its ugly vines and flowers. Suddenly I slammed the glass down on the table. I got up, went to the kitchen, and returned with a small step ladder, the one I had used that morning to change a lightbulb in the ceiling. I pushed the ladder close to the wall. Then I took two steps up the ladder.

Examining a place where the paper had puckered near the ceiling, I slipped my fingers beneath it—then with one sharp tug, I ripped it from the wall. I stood for a moment looking at a large chuck of ragged wallpaper I held in my hand, as if I'd no idea how it had gotten there. Then I let it go and watched it drift to the floor and settle in the dust.

Just below I found another loose piece. It, too, came off easily. It was smaller than the first, but just as satisfying. It joined the other piece on the floor.

I dislodged more and more pieces. Most gave little resistance to my tugs and pulls. They seemed to have been waiting for me to come along and free them. It felt good—like pulling dead skin off your sunburned body; exposing the healthy pink skin beneath it. I couldn't stop.

The air was soon filled with gritty dust and dirt and smells of musty wallpaper paste, decades old. Crude shapes of circles, squares and triangles began growing on the floor surrounding the ladder. Others resembled long fat ribbons, their torn edges bright against the old wallpaper. Each one was examined, then discarded and soon forgotten. When I could no longer reach loose pieces, I moved a few feet and began again, stripping off the offensive wallpaper, gaining momentum as I went.

Eventually I had to go back to the kitchen to get a putty knife from the box of tools I'd left by the back door. I used it to pry up ends of the more stubborn pieces, but it took little effort. Within an hour the wall was clear of wallpaper. What remained was a once-white wall turned gray, and several areas of rust colored stains where the roof had leaked. I thought it looked beautiful.

It was one a.m.

Dolly had at first alternated between sitting and standing in the middle of the room as she watched me, keeping her eyes on my every movement, trying to figure out what I was doing; but then she finally gave up on my madness and went to the kitchen where she laid down to sleep by the porch door.

I moved to the second wall. As I laid it bare, I began to weep again. I had been wrong. I wasn't empty. Instead I had just been reduced to one feeling. It was love.

Chapter 24

I began thinking about all those people I cared about so deeply. I cried for my mother, who wanted to care for babies, but was denied. I wept for her short life and all the things she could have had with her children.

I cried for Janet. She had loved the creek as much as I did. It was there she'd first learned to love science. She would often go there to pick wildflowers, look for new insect specimens, or gather rocks for her rock collection. But she'd given up her dreams of becoming an environmentalist for a husband who in the end betrayed her.

I cried for Charlie, for the choices he'd made, and all the life he could have lived.

I cried for Nora, the only woman I had ever loved.

I thought of baby Sam and cried for a brother I'd never known, wondering again what he would've have been if he had grown up. Maybe he would have married the County Dairy Queen, gotten a blue ribbon for his prize bull at the fair, or expanded the orchard to include cherries and peaches. Or maybe…just maybe…he would have grown up to be something entirely different, like me.

And I cried for my father, who had lived a life of such bitterness that it robbed him of the ability to show love even to his own family.

It was two a.m. when I finished the second wall. I had stopped crying again. I sent up a silent prayer for all the pain those people had suffered and told myself to let it go. I was exhausted, but I had more to do.

I stood looking at the two remaining walls. They should be fairly easy to do. The space on one wall was mostly taken up by the large fireplace and built-in bookshelves. The other had two windows in the middle. I moved my ladder and began again.

When I got to the last wall with the windows, I climbed the ladder and looked across the tops of heavy gold brocade drapes laden with layers of dirt. I took them down and piled them in the middle of the room, sneezing from all the dust and dirt they expelled.

Just after four a.m. I stood in the middle of the living room surveying the chaos I had created. I was covered in sweat and grime. Little pieces of wallpaper stuck to my skin and hair. Thick dust filled the air. The smell of old paste was almost nauseating.

Piles of dead roses littered the floor, sat on the edges of bookshelves and windowsills; were heaped on the pile of drapes in the middle of the room, and hung from the arms of chairs. I let the putty knife drop to the floor. Drained, I went upstairs and fell into an exhausted sleep on top of the quilt, fully clothed.

At nine a.m., Janet arrived.

Neither Dolly nor I had heard her car pull in. The shock of her scream woke us both.

"Patrick! What the hell have you done?"

I jumped up. Sunlight flooded the room. I had forgotten about Janet coming that morning. I should've stayed up and started cleaning up the mess last night. I went to the top of the stairs. Another time I might have looked comical with my hair standing on end, dirt covering my face and arms, and rumpled clothes. I began brushing off bits of wallpaper still stuck to my shirt. Janet was not amused.

"My God, Patrick! We're supposed to be getting the house ready to sell, not demolishing it!"

"Hold on, Sis—"

"No, you hold on. What were you thinking making a mess like this? It will take days to fix this."

Chapter 24

"I was just thinking—"

"No you weren't thinking or you would have realized you should've consulted me about this first."

"I know it looks bad—"

"You're damn right about that! It looks like a bomb went off in here."

"Listen, Janet. It's just that it looked old and dreary. How long has that wallpaper been up there, do you think?" I said as I made my way down the stairs. "Long before you and I were around. Who knows, maybe it was something Grandma Crabtree put up. No one would want a living room that looked like it did. The wallpaper was coming loose all over the place."

"Couldn't we have just gotten new paste and glued it all back down?"

"It still would've looked dirty and faded, and frankly, old-fashioned."

Just when I could feel her beginning to simmer down, she went over and sat in the chair. Her eyes landed on the whisky bottle and half full glass. "Was all this just some drunken rage, Patrick?" she asked, her angry eyes full of blame.

Hell if I knew. I still hadn't worked all that out in my head as yet. "I assure you, Janet, it wasn't," I said, though I couldn't be sure of anything right at that moment.

"Look, Janet, I'm going to clean it all up."

"Damn straight about that."

"And I want you to go home. Take the day off. On Friday when you come back it will all be done."

"I won't be back until Saturday. Friday I have to take Annie to have her wisdom teeth taken out."

"Okay then. That will work. So, what color do you want me to paint it? What would brighten this room up and make it more attractive to buyers?" She sat quietly for a moment, so I added, "We want it move in ready, right?"

Janet got up from her chair and looked around. After a moment I decided to use the old trump card. I asked, "What color would mom have liked?"

"Yellow," she said almost in a whisper. "Mom would have loved yellow."

"Okay, yellow it is," I said with all the cheer I could muster. "I'll clean this up, and then head to the hardware store to buy the prettiest yellow I can find."

Her shoulders slumped.

"And Janet is it okay if I throw out those awful drapes so we can have some more light in here?"

"Whatever," she said, and left.

25

I fed Dolly and let her out. While the coffee brewed I stood in the middle of the living room surveying the mess I'd created. I saw the whisky bottle and half full glass on the side table and took both to the kitchen emptying the contents down the sink.

I started gathering up what I would need: broom, dustpan, bucket, sponge, a large box of garbage bags, and a wheelbarrow. Filling my mug I returned to the living room and decided the first order of the day would be to haul those awful drapes out to the dumpster. I piled them into the wheelbarrow and they soon joined all the other items we once thought valuable and now deemed worthless. Before long it would all be hauled away and good riddance.

Now I had room to work. I began the slow process of ridding the living room of all the debris from last night's….what? I still wasn't sure. As I filled bags with wallpaper scraps I began to see a room emerge free of clutter, and whatever the reason, I knew I had done the right thing. I used the broom to sweep down cobwebs, and a wet sponge to wash the walls, windowsills, and shelves of dust. Four hours and two pots of coffee later, the room was ready to paint. The last thing I did was push the few remaining pieces of furniture into the middle of the room and carry the ladder back in and lean it against a wall.

I went upstairs and took a long, overdue shower. As the hot water washed over me and down the drain, I felt I was freeing myself of debris as well. Afterwards I left in the orchard truck and went to town to buy paint. I'd decided to have dinner at Sally's Café and try to relax for a while. It was only five o'clock, but it had been a long day.

That night I slept better than I had in weeks.

Monday morning I was up early. After a quick breakfast of toast and jam I began rolling primer onto the walls. It was amazing how just changing the dingy gray back to white brightened up the whole space. It took me a couple hours to complete the job. While I let the primer dry, I took Dolly for a walk.

I didn't want to take the time to go all the way to the creek, so we played a few rounds of fetch the ball, and then began a slow amble down rows of apple trees. The grass had gotten quite tall. My dad would have had it all mowed by now. The apples had grown and now were more easily seen. It looked like there would still be a few good apples despite the hard frost. I enjoyed looking at the apple trees and knew I'd never look at an orchard in quite the same way again.

Tuesday. Something was different. I normally hated painting, but that morning I couldn't wait to get started. I poured yellow paint into the paint tray and picked up the roller. I hoped this color would please Janet. I was sorry I had upset her, but it hadn't been intentional. I didn't want any hard feelings between us.

And something else was different. As I rolled tray after tray of yellow paint onto the walls, I finally realized what it was. The anger was gone—replaced by what? Acceptance, maybe. Had I finally been able to accept the things I couldn't change? It was a strange feeling; I hoped it would last. I was ready to feel differently about myself and my life.

As I painted, my thoughts drifted to Nora. I had blamed her for not living her life, but hadn't I done the very same thing? My daily life rarely changed. I never did anything that I could get excited about. Everything seemed to take more energy than I was willing to expend. But these weeks on the farm I had woken up with a feeling of possibility for what I might do each day. I looked forward to going to the creek with Dolly. When was the last time I had looked forward to anything? I was beginning to see things more clearly. Even the smallest things had brought me pleasure—the crazy chickens, watching the cows resting under the trees chewing their cud, the little apples forming on the trees, the sunsets over the barn, Dolly's soft snores as she settled down beside me at night. I hadn't really given up on life; I'd just put it on a shelf somewhere and forgotten about it. By early afternoon I had completed the last coat of paint. I left everything to clean up later. I packed a late lunch and a thermos of coffee. Dolly and I headed to the creek. This time I didn't take my notebook. I wanted to sit and listen to nature and "just be." I knew I'd be leaving it all behind soon.

Wednesday morning I thought things were beginning to take shape. Janet had called and asked me how it was going and to remind me she wouldn't be there until Saturday. She always took a couple days to get over being angry. Her voice was still tight. Knowing her home situation I tried not to let it bother me. I assured her that everything was coming along nicely and that I thought she would be happy with the results.

In the morning light I could see I still needed to do some work. The windows were filthy. I wondered how long it had been since anyone had washed them. And now without the heavy curtains it was easy to see how dirty and threadbare the carpet was once I removed the tarps. I didn't think it would clean up well even if I rented a carpet cleaner. I went to the wall and pulled up a small corner of carpeting. Hardwood. Ah, now that was good news. I pulled it back even farther. So far it looked good. I made a decision; I would rip it all out and stack it on top of the dumpster.

It was hard work and the day was hot. Even with the windows open I perspired profusely. I used a utility knife to cut the carpet and hauled it out in chunks. The dirt and tracked-in sand fell from the carpet and covered the floor. It took a lot longer than I had thought it would. After I finished removing it I decided to take a break out on the porch with a glass of lemonade.

On the porch table the box of letters still sat where I had left them. I hadn't finished reading them, though there was only a handful left. I didn't know if I should even bother. My mood had improved so much; did I really want to risk something that might upset me? But I'm nothing if not curious. It didn't feel right to leave the job unfinished. I guess I was in it to the end. I picked up the last letters and looked at the return addresses.

There were five letters left. Three from Grandma Olmstead to Mom, and one from a friend of mom's thanking her for a birthday present. The last one was from Aunt Edna with a return address in Oregon. It was written to my father in September, 1948.

I pulled out the folded piece of paper and read it slowly, letting the words sink in and take root. If I had read this a few days ago I would've been angry, but now all I felt was sadness.

Chapter 25

September 28, 1948

Dear Samuel,

I read your letter and felt your disappointment, but you've done the right thing, as hard as it was. I know you put your all into that mechanic shop, working years after you got back from the war to save the money for it. But you couldn't' have kept up the shop and the farm both. Mother needs you, and father would have wanted the farm to stay in the family.

You will be rewarded for all your unselfishness. Find yourself a good woman to marry. A farm is a wonderful place to raise a family, don't you think?

Love,

Your sister, Edna

So there it was. I knew that Grandpa Crabtree had died in 1948. Dad must have felt pressured to give up his mechanic shop and take over the farm and look after his mother. But there must have been other choices. I wasn't there, and I know it couldn't have been easy, but couldn't he have sold the farm and moved Grandma into town? Or couldn't Aunt Edna, who had no right to tell him what to do—all the way from Oregon, no less—have sent for Grandma so she could live with her? I mean, what difference did it make to Aunt Edna anyway if dad had kept his mechanic shop?

The farm was his father's life, but it didn't have to be his. Maybe he could have waited until grandma passed, then sold the farm and started a new mechanic shop. What would have stopped him then? Was there still an obligation to his parents to keep farming even after both of them were gone? This was a case of letting others dictate your life from the grave. Something I vowed not to let happen to me.

My dad had been a great mechanic. All the neighbors came to him for help. I know he would've done well if he'd just stuck to his original plans, but he didn't, and we all paid for it in the disappointment he carried with him his whole life. No wonder he didn't think I should do anything different, why he denied me my chance, because that might mean he would have to admit that maybe he'd been wrong in his own choices.

I folded the letter and put it back in the envelope, gathered up the rest, and returned them to the box. I shook my head. I thought of all the letters and photographs I'd discovered over the span of weeks. Maybe it would have been better to have found them all in one box. Let all that hurt and pain settle on me in one big swoop. But that may have proved to be too much to take in. Better to have gotten it all in smaller doses.

If I had known these things when I was younger would it have made things any different in my life? I had a lot of thinking to do. The last thing I wanted to do was to follow in my dad's footsteps.

I went back to the living room and began mopping the floor, thinking about how one person's decisions could affect so many people.

It took several buckets full of water to finally get the floor clean, but when it was finished it looked good. Then I washed the living room windows, inside and out. Lastly, I moved all the furniture back and cleaned up, declaring myself done.

That night was beautiful. There was a slight chill in the air. Stars were in abundance in the cloudless sky. At dusk I built a campfire and sat watching flames catch hold of the wood I'd piled into the pit, listening to the snapping sounds of twigs burning, and following the sparks as they ascended skyward. Beside me Dolly lay intently working on her rawhide chewy. I was very tired, but it was a "good" tired.

Thinking back over the past few weeks Janet and I sure had covered a lot of territory, from cleaning out the house, to getting rid of the chickens and cows, the auction, and selling the land. If I had known we were going to tackle all that in the beginning I think I might have gotten back in my car and left!

Tomorrow was Thursday. Monday I was due back at work at nine a.m. I rested my hand on Dolly's head, feeling the strength of her jaw muscles as she chewed. The comfort I felt when I stroked her silky ears was something I was sorely going to miss. I still hadn't decided what I was going to do with her.

I sat back and watched as darkness set in. Several bats flew out of the upper barn windows on their way out for the nightly hunt. An orchestra of frogs performed music for the fireflies as they weaved and danced their way through the tall grass, their tiny lanterns winking —lights on, lights off.

I finally began to feel my body relax. I'd brought a couple things with me. First I took Aunt Edna's letter to dad from my pocket. I read it one last time. It was time. Time to end the obligations of the Crabtree family. I held it above the flames, then without another thought I let it drop into the fire. It disappeared for good, taking with it the pain of not living your own life, of not being who you were meant to be.

For another hour I sat thinking about the past month. I knew I'd never be back to this place again, but memories had a way of traveling with you, whether you wanted them to or not. Janet had been right. She'd told me to remember the good times. I needed to stop letting the painful ones continue to drag me through the muck and rocks of life. But it would be up to me. I needed to replace the painful memories with good ones.

When I thought of dad, there would be few good things to remember. But all I needed was one to start. I finally thought of one. A magazine in a sock drawer.

With that I took a deep breath and retrieved the picture of my father and his war buddy, Patrick 'Paddy' Murphy, from my jacket. There they were, smiles on their faces, arms around each other's shoulders, not knowing what life would bring them. For dad, bitterness and regret. For Patrick, hardly any life at all. I'd been thinking about what I wanted to do with this photograph. There were plenty of other photographs of dad in the box. But this one? They seemed stuck in time. Looking at this photo brought only painful thoughts of both of them. In the end I decided they needed to be set free and I needed a new beginning. I picked up the photo and held it to the firelight.

"Patrick, I never knew you, or even knew of you," I said, "but my dad saw something in you that was good. He chose you for a friend and thought enough of you that he named me after you. I wish I could've known you and what you thought of my dad. There's so much about him that I'll never understand. I wish you both could've lived your own dreams. I've decided the best way to honor you both is to live my life, live it in a way that it isn't wasted on regrets. It's time for you both to rest in peace."

I dropped the photograph into the fire.

With that, I leaned back in my chair, looked up at the stars, and listened to the owls call from tree to tree. Soon I fell into a peaceful sleep, full of dreams.

26

I woke with a kink in my neck and my clothes damp with dew. The sun was just on the horizon displaying pale colors of pink and yellow. The robins were beginning their morning songs. Dolly lay curled into a tight ball next to the campfire, which was now just ashes. Thin wisps of smoke rose to the sky, my spirits rising with them.

I stood and stretched, Dolly doing the same. Then she did a quick hard shake. I walked to the house. Dolly picked up her rawhide chewy and followed close behind. While the coffee brewed and Dolly ate, I took a hot shower and warmed myself. I gathered my toiletries and went to the bedroom where I packed them in my duffle bag along with my clothes. I carried them out to the car, placing them in the back.

Returning to the house I picked up an empty box from the porch and headed back upstairs. I emptied the contents of my desk into the box, along with all my high school note books and a few mementoes. I picked up the two yearbooks I'd found in the closet. I'd enjoy looking through them later and think about all the good times Buddy, Charlie and I had had together. I still planned on making new memories with Buddy. I put them in the box. Next I folded the quilt my mom had made me and carried it all down to the car. Dolly lay between the house and the car, head on her paws, eyes fixed on me as I went back and forth.

I packed up my computer and a few books and set them by the back door. I poured myself a mug of coffee and put the rest in the thermos. From the back pack I pulled out my notebook and tore out a clean sheet of paper. Sitting down with my coffee, I wrote Janet a letter.

Saturday morning Janet walked into the house, letting the screen door fall shut behind her. She wondered where Patrick had gotten himself off to. Maybe he needed something from town. Then she saw it—the living room. It had been transformed. The room was filled with a luscious glow. It felt warm and comforting and invigorating all at the same time. She stood in the middle and did a full circle. She had been wrong to be mad at Patrick. This was wonderful. Mom would have loved it.

She went to the kitchen and filled the coffee pot with water and coffee, then stood by the kitchen window that looked out over the farm while she waited for it to finish. She could see the lane and the orchard with its few apples. There were birds gathered near a puddle in the driveway drinking from last night's rain. It all seemed so peaceful; so quiet.

Where was Patrick anyway?

She decided to take her coffee to the porch and wait for him. Then she turned and saw them; the bundle of letters on top of a box, the box of photos, and a letter on the table.

She sat down and laced her fingers around the coffee mug. An uneasy feeling came over her. First she opened the photo box and looked at the stack of pictures. On top was the picture of baby Sam.

Chapter 26

She smiled. She had wanted it, but never asked Patrick for it. The rest were family photos, mostly of when they were kids growing up together and a few of mom and dad. In a Manilla envelope Patrick had placed the rest of the photos. He wrote on it "Unknown…do what you want with these." She put them all back in the box and picked up a note he had put in with the photos. He told her he would make her a copy of the photo of mom with the watermelon and asked if she would make him a copy of baby Sam and the one with mom and dad when Sam was a newborn.

The bundle of letters was tied together with string. A small note told her they were from Grandma Olmstead to mom. Patrick thought she would enjoy reading them. He'd left the other letters, the ones from people they didn't know, in the box, but like the pictures she could just throw them out if she didn't want them.

She picked up the letter Patrick had written. Sadness came over her. She knew then that he had left. She refilled her mug and went to the porch to read it.

Dear Sis,

I hope you like the living room. The color is called Golden Glow. Quite appropriate don't you think? It sure is pretty when the sun shines in through the windows.

As you can probably tell, I've decided to leave. We've both done as much as we can do here. It's time to call the realtor and put the house up for sale. Both of us need to get on with our lives. I won't be far. I promise, I'll just be a phone call away if you need me.

By the time you have read this I will have quit my job. Don't worry. I have money saved and soon there will be money coming from Henry and Junior. I have two months left on my lease for my apartment, but I won't be renewing it. I know

now I'll never be happy in a big city. I realized I had never really appreciated the farm until now. I just want to wake up in the morning to sounds of nature. I plan to sell my car and get a pickup truck and a small camper trailer. I'm going to be a vagabond for a while, until I decide what I'm going to do next. There's a lot of this country I've never seen.

For now I'm headed up to see Buddy and Sarah in Traverse City. I've never been to his flight school and he just bought a new plane. Maybe I can convince him to take me up for a spin.

I just wanted to say, Sis, that I'm very glad to have you for a sister. You've always been there for me and worried about everyone else. Now it's time to think about yourself for a change.

Love,
Patrick

P. S. Dolly is with me.

Janet put down the letter. She sat on the porch, letting the morning sun warm her. She heard the call of an eagle and wondered if it had made a nest in the woods. Maybe the morels were ready to be picked. She thought about her mom's rosebush. It probably should be watered again. The last time she checked, it had gotten some new leaves. After a few moments she took her coffee with her and returned to the living room. She stood in the shimmering light and let peace settle over her like a warm embrace. She began imaging her favorite reading chair pushed up beside the fireplace on a cold winter night, her many books lined up on mom's bookshelves, and her favorite watercolor of a marsh hanging over the mantel. The corners of her mouth turned up slightly.

"Perhaps," she thought.

ACKNOWLEDGMENTS

Thank you to all my first readers, Myrna Brenner, Jan Johnson, and to the members of the Literati writers group from Adelaide, Australia, with special thanks to Caz, Dimity, and May-Kuan. You are all people with very busy lives and I appreciate the time you gave to this project. Your advice and encouragement went a long way into making this book happen.

And many thanks to Herbie's Café for allowing me to hangout every morning back in my little corner writing and drinking tons of coffee.

May good things come to all who have given so much.

Susan

www.ingramcontent.com/pod-product-compliance
Lightning Source LLC
Chambersburg PA
CBHW030628120726
47904CB00006B/2082